THE TEAPOT KILLER

Churchill and Pemberley Mystery Book 9

EMILY ORGAN

Copyright © 2025 by Emily Organ

All rights reserved.

emilyorgan.com

Emily Organ has asserted her right under the Copyright, Designs and Patents Act 1988 to be identified as the author of this work.

All characters and events in this publication, other than those clearly in the public domain, are fictitious and any resemblance to real persons, living or dead, is purely coincidental.

ISBN 978-1-7384465-7-5

This book is copyright material and must not be copied, reproduced, transferred, distributed, leased, licensed or publicly performed or used in any way except as specifically permitted in writing by the publisher, as allowed under the terms and conditions under which it was purchased or as strictly permitted by applicable copyright law. Any unauthorised distribution or use of this text may be a direct infringement of the author's and publisher's rights and those responsible may be liable in law accordingly.

The Churchill and Pemberley Series

Tragedy at Piddleton Hotel
Murder in Cold Mud
Puzzle in Poppleford Wood
Trouble in the Churchyard
Wheels of Peril
The Poisoned Peer
Fiasco at the Jam Factory
Disaster at the Christmas Dinner
The Teapot Killer
Christmas Calamity at the Vicarage (novella)

Chapter One

'What are you two doing here?' asked Mrs Thonnings. She wore a wide-brimmed hat decorated with spring flowers. 'I thought you'd be the last people Inspector Mappin would invite to his retirement party.'

Annabel Churchill took in a breath and forced a smile. 'How nice of you to point it out, Mrs Thonnings.' She surveyed the gathering on the sunny village green. 'He's invited the entire population of Compton Poppleford, and I've never been one to turn down a celebration.'

'I often turn them down,' said Churchill's assistant, Doris Pemberley. 'But I made an exception for today.'

'Then we're grateful to you for gracing us with your presence,' said Churchill. She glanced around. 'Are there any refreshments here?'

'Oh yes,' said Mrs Thonnings. 'Mrs Honeypear has set up her refreshments tent.' She pointed to the far end of the green where a red and white striped marquee stood, decorated with colourful bunting.

'A tent for refreshments?' Churchill felt her heart give a joyful skip.

'Yes, Mrs Honeypear is very organised,' said Mrs Thonnings. 'And she's done such a marvellous job with the tea rooms since she took over.'

'I concur with that,' said Churchill. 'Lovely cakes.'

'Incredible cakes,' agreed Mrs Thonnings. 'In fact, I'm delighted her husband ran off with a circus performer from Bournemouth.'

Churchill startled. 'Is that what happened? How awful. Why are you delighted about it, Mrs Thonnings?'

'Because that's what made Mrs Honeypear buy the tea rooms. She threw herself into the project and the entire village has benefited.'

'I see. And if she'd remained married to her scoundrel husband, the tea rooms would have continued to languish. Out of the darkness comes light. And things really did go downhill at the tea rooms. I recall eating a piece of shortbread there which was indistinguishable from a piece of cardboard. It was indigestible, too. In fact, the effects of it lasted—'

'Oh, look,' interrupted Pemberley. 'Someone important is arriving.'

A large, shiny motor car had pulled up alongside the village green. The chauffeur got out and opened the doors for a red-moustached police officer and a lady with an upturned nose and a large mauve hat.

'Chief Inspector Llewellyn-Dalrymple,' said Churchill. 'And that lady must be his wife.'

'She looks very serious,' said Pemberley.

'That's because she's married to Llewellyn-Dalrymple. I can't imagine there being much lightness and fun in their household.'

'She enjoys her needlework,' said Mrs Thonnings. 'In fact, she's a regular visitor to my haberdashery shop.'

'Who's the other chap with them?' asked Churchill. A

sharp-featured uniformed inspector had also got out of the car and was surveying the scene from beneath the peak of his cap.

'That's Inspector Kendall,' said Mrs Thonnings. 'He's Inspector Mappin's replacement. He's come all the way from Salisbury. Apparently, he was promoted quickly there, and he's very ambitious. But I think it's a shame. I'm going to miss Inspector Mappin.'

'I suppose I will too,' said Churchill. 'Even though he was hapless at times.' She felt unsure how well her detective agency was going to work with the new inspector. Judging by the faint scowl on his face, she didn't have high hopes for a cordial relationship. 'Let's cheer ourselves up in the refreshments tent,' she said.

Chapter Two

Inside the refreshments tent, long trestle tables were stacked with a colourful array of cakes, biscuits and sandwiches.

'Goodness, Pemberley,' said Churchill, her mouth watering. 'I don't know where to start!'

Mrs Honeypear stood at the far end of the tent pouring out tea from an enormous teapot. She wore a red bow in her fair, wavy hair and greeted them with a wide smile as they approached. 'Tea, ladies?'

'Yes please,' said Churchill. 'You must need a bit of strength to wield that teapot.'

'I suppose I do,' she chuckled. 'It holds nine pints and, if I pour carefully, I can get thirty cups out of it.' She deftly filled three delicate china teacups and invited them to help themselves to milk from a blue and white milk jug.

'Which cakes do you recommend, Mrs Honeypear?' asked Churchill. 'You have so much choice here.'

'The simnel cake,' she said. 'Because it's Easter time and it's very popular. So have a slice now, ladies, before it runs out.'

'Oh, I love simnel cake!' said Mrs Thonnings. 'It's my favourite!'

Churchill bit into her slice and enjoyed the rich fruits and sweet marzipan. 'This cake is perfect.'

Pemberley nodded, her mouth full.

Mrs Thonnings bit into her slice. Then her eyebrows shot up her forehead and her eyes grew as large as saucers.

'Lovely, isn't it?' said Churchill.

Mrs Thonnings made a strange sound from the back of her throat.

'Are you alright, Mrs Thonnings? You're not choking, are you?'

Mrs Thonnings pointed to her mouth as she tried to gulp down the cake. Churchill exchanged a baffled glance with Pemberley and took a sip of tea

'That's my simnel cake!' said Mrs Thonnings as soon as she'd finished her mouthful. 'Mrs Honeypear has made my simnel cake!'

'*Your* simnel cake?' asked Churchill.

'Yes! My grandmother's secret recipe which was handed down to my mother, then me. It has the secret ingredient in it. I can taste it!'

'What is the secret ingredient?'

'I can't say. It's a closely guarded secret!'

'Are you sure you're not mistaken, Mrs Thonnings?'

'Absolutely sure!' She marched over to Mrs Honeypear.

'Oh dear, Pembers,' muttered Churchill. 'She's going to cause a scene.' She shifted uncomfortably from one foot to the other.

'Where did you get the recipe for that simnel cake from?' demanded Mrs Thonnings.

'It's my grandmother's recipe,' said Mrs Honeypear.

'Nonsense!'

Mrs Honeypear took a step back. 'Excuse me? It's not nonsense at all.'

'Yes, it is! Because this simnel cake has been baked to my grandmother's recipe.'

'I'm afraid it hasn't, Mrs Thonnings. And I don't appreciate you being confrontational in my refreshments tent.'

Churchill went over to them, hoping to calm things down. 'I'm sure this is just a misunderstanding, Mrs Thonnings,' she said. 'After all, one simnel cake tastes very similar to another.'

'No, it doesn't!' said Mrs Thonnings.

'That's right,' said Mrs Honeypear. 'It doesn't!'

'Very well.' Churchill stepped away again. 'I shan't get involved then.'

'I haven't seen Oswald for a while,' Pemberley said to her. 'Shall we look for him?'

'Yes, that's an excellent idea, Pembers.'

They stepped out of the tent, relieved to leave the argument behind them. They strolled around the village green looking for Pemberley's scruffy, wiry-haired dog.

People chatted merrily around them and children played. Everyone was dressed in their Sunday best and enjoying the first warm day of the year.

'There are lots of policemen here,' remarked Pemberley.

'That's because it's Inspector Mappin's retirement party.'

'I'm worried all the criminals will get up to no good while there are no bobbies on the beat.'

'Oh, I wouldn't worry, Pemberley. We don't have many criminals here in Compton Poppleford. And besides, with most of the Dorset Constabulary in attendance here, we know we're as safe as houses! Oh look, there's Oswald. He's made a friend.'

The little dog was cantering around with another scruffy-looking canine.

'It's so lovely to see him making a friend,' said Pemberley. 'I do worry about him sometimes, he seems such a loner. I often think a little friend would make him so much happier. And look, he's found one!'

'I wonder who the other dog belongs to?' said Churchill.

A tall, thin, bespectacled lady headed towards them. She bore a striking resemblance to Pemberley. 'Are you the owners of that dog?' she asked, pointing at Oswald.

'Yes. I am,' said Pemberley, proudly.

'Oh good. I'm so happy Whisker's made a little friend.'

'That's just what I was saying!' said Pemberley. 'Isn't it lovely to see them playing together?'

'Yes, it is. What's your dog called?'

'Oswald. He's a Spanish Water Dog with a touch of terrier and a splash of spaniel.'

'Is he indeed? He's a delightful animal. Whisker is a Portuguese Water Dog. He's also got a bit of terrier and spaniel in him, too.'

'Well, I never!' said Pemberley. 'No wonder they both get on so well. Do you and Whisker live here in the village?'

'Yes, we do.'

'Well, I can't believe we've never met before,' said Pemberley.

'Me neither. My name is Miss Winifred Applethorn. I'm the new librarian.'

'Are you? I love books!' said Pemberley.

'And so do I!' said Miss Applethorn.

As the two ladies talked about dogs and books,

Churchill found herself being excluded from the conversation. She glanced around, looking for someone else to talk to. Then she spotted people eating ice creams. She decided to find out where they'd got them from.

It wasn't long before she saw the white and lemon ice cream cart. The proprietor wore a crisp white coat and hat.

Churchill's steps faltered as she neared the cart and realised who the ice cream seller was. She was a tall, broad lady with long grey hair framing a stern, square face.

Mrs Higginbath. Churchill's nemesis.

'Good afternoon, Mrs Churchill,' she said.

'Good afternoon, Mrs Higginbath. I didn't know you were in the business of selling ice cream these days.'

'Well, you know now.'

'Wonderful. What flavours do you have?'

'Vanilla.'

'Lovely. And what else?'

'Nothing else. Just vanilla.'

'Oh, I see. Is there a choice of cone?'

'No. Everybody gets the same,' said Mrs Higginbath.

'So there's not a great deal of choice.'

'The choice is simple, Mrs Churchill. Either you buy an ice cream or you don't.'

'Succinctly put, Mrs Higginbath. I'd like an ice cream, please.'

'That will be sixpence.'

'Sixpence?'

'Yes.'

'But I paid twopence for an ice cream on Weymouth beach last year.'

'This isn't Weymouth, Mrs Churchill.'

'No. You're right about that.' She rummaged about in her purse for a sixpence. 'This is an expensive ice cream.'

'I have high running costs.'

'I see. Now watch how you handle my coin,' she said as she handed it over.

'And what do you mean by that, Mrs Churchill?'

'There was that business of you pocketing library fines, wasn't there?'

Mrs Higginbath's expression darkened. 'It was a false accusation! The head librarian was looking for an excuse to get rid of me, so he accused me of stealing. And anyway, selling ice cream is far more fulfilling than working in that dusty old library.'

'Yes, I'm sure it is. Here you are out in the fresh air, serving ice creams at Inspector Mappin's retirement party on this lovely, sunny day. Life doesn't really get any better than this, does it, Mrs Higginbath?'

'No, it doesn't.' Mrs Higginbath scowled. 'I've never been happier.'

Chapter Three

'You found an ice cream, Mrs Churchill,' said Pemberley.

'I didn't find it. I had to part with sixpence for it! A daylight robbery. Mrs Higginbath is selling them if you're feeling brave enough to buy one. What happened to your new friend?'

'Miss Applethorn? She's gone to the refreshments tent. She wants to get a cup of tea before the speeches and the Morris dancers.'

'Speeches? Morris dancers?' Churchill groaned. 'I might have to make my excuses before then.' She caught sight of Chief Inspector Llewellyn-Dalrymple close by. 'Let's go and speak to Llewellyn-Dalrymple, Pemberley. We haven't seen him since Christmas, and I'm sure he'll be delighted to be reminded of us.'

His red moustache bristled as they approached. 'Oh, it's you two,' he said. 'The two ladies who go about interfering with police business.'

'That description is a little unkind, Chief Inspector,'

said Churchill. 'We've actually solved quite a few crimes now.'

He gave a snort. 'This is my wife, Mrs Llewellyn-Dalrymple.'

The lady with the mauve hat and upturned nose held out a limp gloved hand for them to shake.

'It's a pleasure to meet you, Mrs Llewellyn-Dalrymple,' said Churchill.

'Likewise.' Her gaze went over Churchill's shoulder to something in the distance.

Churchill turned back to the chief inspector. 'This is a momentous day for you, saying goodbye to one of your longest-serving inspectors.'

'Yes, I suppose it is. Mappin's ready for it, though. He's more than ready to be put out to pasture.'

'Is he?'

'Oh yes. He disagrees with me, of course. But I don't believe any man is the best judge of when it's his time to go. Often it takes someone else to point it out to him.' He took his wife's arm. 'Anyway, let's get a cup of tea, dear, before I have to make my speech.'

Churchill watched them leave. 'If I understand him correctly, Pembers, he's suggesting Mappin doesn't actually want to retire. I didn't realise it was being forced on him. Did you?'

Pemberley shook her head. 'There's Mrs Mappin over there,' she said. 'Perhaps we can find out more from her.'

'Good idea.'

Mrs Mappin had grey curly hair and wore a floral tea dress which was a little too tight in the bodice.

'What an emotional day this must be for you, Mrs Mappin,' said Churchill.

The inspector's wife gave a sad nod. 'Yes, I suppose you

could put it like that. I have no idea what my husband is going to do with his time in retirement.'

'What does he enjoy doing? Fishing? Stamp collecting? Gardening?'

'He did like tennis, but then his knees began playing up. The only thing he really enjoys is being a police inspector.'

'Oh dear. Why is he retiring then?'

'He was told to by the powers that be.' She pursed her lips.

'Who? Specifically?'

'Well, his boss, of course.'

'Chief Inspector Llewellyn-Dalrymple?'

She nodded.

'He's forcing your husband to take early retirement?'

'Yes.'

'But why? If Inspector Mappin has got many years left in him yet, then there's no need for him to retire now, is there? Especially if he enjoys his job so much.'

'I think the chief inspector wants to get some fresh blood in. But it's my poor husband who suffers. And me as well, of course. It's only going to get worse. After today, my husband will be sitting around at home with a face like a wet weekend. He'll be twiddling his thumbs and getting under my feet, and I can't see either of us being happy about it.'

'No, that doesn't sound like a lot of fun. Retirement is supposed to be enjoyable. When my dear departed husband, Chief Inspector Churchill, retired, he was sad to stop his work but was looking forward to a well-earned rest. Although I'm afraid to say he didn't enjoy his retirement for long because he died six months later.'

'Oh, I really don't want my husband to die in six months' time!' said Mrs Mappin.

'I'm sure he won't,' said Churchill, now wishing she hadn't related her own experience.

'I've tried my hardest to make Chief Inspector Llewellyn-Dalrymple change his mind,' said Mrs Mappin. 'But he won't listen to me. I even spoke to his superior, Superintendent Trowelbank. But he told me he doesn't get involved in these decisions.' She shrugged. 'What can I do? My poor dear husband is in despair about it all.'

A ringing bell interrupted them.

'Oh, it's time for the speeches,' said Mrs Mappin. 'I'd better go and stand at my husband's side and look happy.'

Everyone gathered in front of a little stage which had been erected on one side of the village green. Chief Inspector Llewellyn-Dalrymple climbed onto it and smiled smugly beneath his red moustache.

'I would like to thank you all for attending this gathering today to celebrate the career of one of the finest police inspectors Compton Poppleford has ever seen,' he said. 'And I'm sure you will join me in wishing Inspector Mappin a long and happy retirement.'

A ripple of applause followed, and a dejected-looking Inspector Mappin stepped onto the stage. His shoulders were slumped and his brown whiskers looked dishevelled.

Chief Inspector Llewellyn-Dalrymple presented him with a certificate and a commemorative watch. After another round of applause had subsided, there were calls for Inspector Mappin to make a speech. He gave a sigh and stepped forward.

'I have very much enjoyed my career with the Compton Poppleford police force,' he said miserably. 'It only seems like yesterday when I joined the force as a young constable under the watchful eye of Inspector Grindlethorpe.' He took off his cap and raised his eyes skyward for a moment. Then he replaced his cap and continued. 'I don't quite know what I'm going to be doing with myself after today. As many of you know, my retirement was not my choice but a suggestion by my superiors.' He gave Chief Inspector Llewellyn-Dalrymple a sharp glance. 'However, I'm extremely grateful to you all for coming here today and showing me your gratitude for my work. I hope to see you all around the village over the coming years.'

He took out a handkerchief and dabbed his eyes. Churchill felt a lump in her throat.

Inspector Mappin gave a little bow, then left the stage as everyone applauded him.

'Jolly good,' said Chief Inspector Llewellyn-Dalrymple, straightening his jacket. The sunlight gleamed on its shiny buttons. 'I would like to introduce you all now to Inspector Kendall. Inspector Mappin's replacement with immediate effect.'

Inspector Kendall marched onto the stage, his chin thrust forward. He saluted the chief inspector and a handful of people gave a cautious applause.

'Thank you, sir, for the welcome. And thank you, all of you gathered here, for welcoming me to your delightful village. As many of you know, I cut my teeth in the Salisbury police force, so you could say I know a thing or two about policing. I know that change is often unpopular, but I'm very excited about coming here and shaking things up a bit.'

Churchill dozed on her feet as Inspector Kendall rambled on like a newly elected politician. Eventually, he stopped and the jangle of bells announced the arrival of the Morris dancers. Everyone moved to form a ring around the eight men dressed in white with red ribbons and sashes and bells strapped to their limbs. A ninth man struck up a jaunty tune on his accordion and the men

The Teapot Killer

began to skip in formation, wielding handkerchiefs and sticks which they knocked together with cheery shouts.

'Aren't they good?' said Mrs Thonnings, sidling up to Churchill during the third dance.

'They're not bad,' said Churchill.

'See that gentleman there with the white moustache? He's a former boyfriend of mine.'

Churchill stifled a gasp. 'Is that so?'

'Mr Cruddle. He was quite adorable. But then his wife wanted to make another go of their marriage.'

'Did you know he was married at the time?'

'Oh yes. He was always very honest about it. I don't mind if my boyfriends are married as long as they're honest about it.'

'I see.'

Churchill wondered if it would be impolite to visit the refreshments tent during the dance. Just as she decided it wouldn't be, an ear-piercing scream shattered the music.

The dancers stopped, and the accordion fell silent. Heads turned and people gasped.

'Murder!' shouted a voice. 'There's been a murder!'

Chapter Four

THE COMMOTION WAS COMING FROM THE REFRESHMENTS tent. Churchill and Pemberley followed the crowd to the tent, which was quickly cordoned off by all the police officers who'd been attending the party. Pemberley held Oswald in her arms to keep him safe from the trampling feet.

Inspector Mappin pushed his way through. 'Move back, everyone!' he called out. 'I'll deal with this.'

He stepped through the police cordon and into the tent.

Churchill's stomach knotted. 'Murder, Pembers? It's chilling.'

A few moments later, Inspector Mappin emerged from the tent with Mrs Honeypear. They were both ashen faced.

'Is there a doctor here?' asked the inspector.

Three gentlemen stepped forward and discussed which one of them should go into the tent.

'Who's been murdered?' called out someone.

'Tell us!' said another.

'I'm unable to say until I have spoken with the next of

kin,' said Inspector Mappin. 'Where's Mrs Llewellyn-Dalrymple?'

Churchill gasped. 'I do believe Mappin has just given it away,' she said. 'The victim must be the chief inspector!'

Mrs Thonnings joined Churchill and Pemberley. 'Isn't this dreadful?' she said. 'They're saying the chief inspector is dead!'

'Excuse me,' Inspector Kendall pushed his way through the crowd, he had a half-eaten ice cream in his hand. 'I'm in charge here,' he said to Mappin. 'You've retired, and I'm the new inspector.'

'Today is my last day,' said Inspector Mappin. 'I've not fully retired until the end of today. And besides, no one can expect you to have a murder as your very first case here in Compton Poppleford. You don't have the knowledge of this village to investigate it properly.'

'I beg your pardon? I cut my teeth in Salisbury. Are you trying to tell me I don't know what I'm doing?'

'Have you ever investigated a murder before, Kendall?'

'I've investigated many serious crimes, Mappin.' He pointed his ice cream at him. 'Now step aside and let me deal with this.'

'Have you ever investigated a murder before?' pressed Inspector Mappin.

'I don't have to go into the details of everything I have and haven't done right now.'

'So you haven't investigated a murder before?'

'I've already told you I'm not discussing it.'

'But if you had investigated a murder before, then you would admit it, wouldn't you?'

'Step aside, Mappin, or I shall—'

'Or you shall what, Kendall? Report me to Chief Inspector Llewellyn-Dalrymple? I'm afraid you can't, because he's dead.'

'Goodness me,' said Mrs Thonnings. 'I had no idea Inspector Mappin could be so feisty. He's quite attractive when he's angry, isn't he?'

Churchill shook her head in dismay. 'I'll pretend I didn't hear you say that, Mrs Thonnings.' She glanced around her. 'I can't say I'm enjoying standing about in this crowd watching police officers argue with each other. Shall we get some air, Pemberley?'

'Definitely.'

The two ladies battled their way out of the throng.

'Well, what an eventful afternoon,' said Churchill. 'Who on earth wanted Chief Inspector Llewellyn-Dalrymple dead?'

As they reached the edge of the village green, they heard someone sobbing on the other side of an oak tree.

'Goodness,' whispered Churchill. 'Can you hear that?'

Pemberley nodded.

They rounded the thick, gnarled trunk to find Mrs Honeypear there in floods of tears.

'Oh goodness, are you all right?' asked Churchill.

'No, I'm not all right. I can't believe what's just happened!'

'It must have been a dreadful shock for you.'

'Yes, it was. I returned to my refreshments tent, and it was just a horrific sight. There was a man lying prostrate on the ground, and my favourite stoneware teapot was in pieces next to him.'

'The enormous teapot which you served us tea from?'

'Yes. It's in bits! I've used it for years—it's my favourite teapot. Everyone tells me they've never tasted tea as good as the tea that's made in that pot.'

Churchill gave this some thought. 'Are you telling me,

Mrs Honeypear, that your stoneware teapot was used to murder the chief inspector?'

She nodded and burst into fresh sobs.

'Goodness me,' said Churchill. 'It must have been quite a blow. Hopefully Chief Inspector Llewellyn-Dalrymple knew very little about it.'

'I don't understand it,' wailed Mrs Honeypear. 'Why murder him in my tent? With my teapot?'

'There, there.' Churchill patted her on the shoulder. 'It must feel very personal, Mrs Honeypear. But I'm sure it's not. The murderer clearly made the most of an opportunity.'

'But why murder the chief inspector?'

'That's a very good question, and I'm sure it's one we're going to be asking a great deal over the coming days. Especially Inspector Mappin—or Inspector Kendall. Who knows who will investigate it? They can't seem to agree between themselves, and there's no one to tell them what to do because he's the one who's been murdered.'

'It's complete anarchy!' cried Mrs Honeypear.

'It may feel like that at the moment, but it will get sorted. The local constabulary may be all at sixes and sevens at the present time, but Miss Pemberley and I will investigate, Mrs Honeypear. Don't you worry.'

Chapter Five

'That was the most eventful retirement party I've ever been to, Pemberley,' said Churchill as she arrived at the office the following morning. She placed a bag of freshly baked goods on Pemberley's desk.

'What's in there?' Pemberley asked.

'Four cinnamon and currant buns.'

'Oh, lovely! I'll get some plates for them and make some tea.'

A short while later, the two ladies settled at their desks and discussed the case over tea and buns.

'It was such a lovely day for the party,' said Churchill. 'The first warm day of the year. Then someone ruined it by hitting Chief Inspector Llewellyn-Dalrymple over the head with an enormous teapot.'

'How did they know it was empty?' asked Pemberley.

'Did it need to be empty?'

'Yes. Quite empty, I think. It would require a lot of strength to wield it while full of tea.'

'Good point.' Churchill ate a mouthful of bun. 'Perhaps the murderer tipped out the tea first. But how did the murderer know Chief Inspector Llewellyn-Dalrymple was going to be in the refreshments tent while everyone was watching the Morris dancers?'

'The murderer must have arranged to meet him there,' said Pemberley.

'Yes. They planned it well. They must have realised there would be no one in the refreshments tent while the Morris dancers were performing. My immediate thought is that Mrs Honeypear is the culprit. It was her tent, her teapot, and she was the one to discover the crime. Did you see her watching the Morris dancers, Pemberley?'

'No, I didn't. But why would she want to murder Chief Inspector Llewellyn-Dalrymple?'

'I don't know. I don't think they even knew each other. And she was rather distressed about her broken teapot, wasn't she? It's unlikely she wanted to cause such chaos in her own refreshments tent. I think she left the tent to watch the Morris dancers, and that's when the murderer struck. Perhaps they went into the tent with Llewellyn-Dalrymple. Did you see who he was with before the Morris dancers began?'

Pemberley shook her head. 'No. But perhaps we should consider Inspector Mappin as a suspect. He could have asked the chief inspector for a quiet word in the refreshments tent. And he has a motive, doesn't he? He didn't want to retire, but Chief Inspector Llewellyn-Dalrymple was forcing him to.'

'He has an excellent motive indeed, Pemberley. Revenge.'

'But I can't believe Inspector Mappin would do such a thing. He's always been a fairly mild-mannered man.'

'Don't forget what his wife said, Pemberley. She told us his forced retirement had driven him to the edge of despair. You and I both know that people can act out of character in those circumstances.'

'He may have been upset about being forced to retire, but why risk spending his entire retirement in prison? Or even worse, being hanged for it?'

'Perhaps if he was on the edge of despair, then he wouldn't have thought so rationally. Maybe he was consumed with rage when he struck his boss with the teapot. However, we should try to think of some other suspects.'

'I don't believe Inspector Mappin did it,' said Pemberley. 'But I can't think of any other suspects.'

'There's only one thing for it, Pembers,' said Churchill, finishing off her currant bun. 'We need to visit the scene of the crime.'

Chapter Six

Churchill and Pemberley stood beneath the large oak tree and surveyed the village green.

'It looks smaller now there are no people on it,' said Pemberley.

'You're right, it does. And it's hard to remember how everything was laid out, isn't it? Anyway, I think the refreshments tent was over there, to the right of the duck pond.'

Oswald trotted ahead of them as they crossed the green. It was another warm sunny day, and the trees were filled with birdsong.

They reached a flattened area of grass. 'I think the tent stood here,' said Churchill. 'But it's difficult to be certain, isn't it?'

Oswald walked around in circles, his nose pressed to the ground. Then he wandered a few more yards and sniffed the ground more intently.

'Is he eating something?' asked Churchill.

'Yes, it looks like it,' said Pemberley. She went over to

her dog and bent down to take a closer look. 'Cake crumbs,' she said.

'Excellent! Then we must be in the right place. Lots of cake crumbs will have been dropped in the refreshments tent.'

Churchill examined the ground and eventually found something. 'Look at this, Pembers. A hole which must have been made by one of the poles supporting the tent. And if I walk over this way… yes, the edge of the tent was here, wasn't it? Here's a hole for another pole. We need to mark this out with something, but I don't know what.'

'Would a ball of wool help?' said Pemberley. 'I have one in my handbag.'

'Yes, that will help enormously, Pemberley! What a great idea.'

A short while later, the outline of the refreshments tent had been marked out with a strand of fuchsia pink wool kept in place with sticks and stones.

Churchill stood in the centre. 'Now we can examine this area of grass for clues.'

They began scouring the ground and Oswald tidied up the cake crumbs.

'There's not a lot here,' said Churchill after a while. 'Mrs Honeypear did a good job of tidying everything away when she packed up her tent.'

'I've found something!' said Pemberley, stooping down to pick it up. 'It's very sharp. I'm relieved Oswald didn't accidentally tread on it. It looks like… a shard from the teapot!'

'Excellent, Pembers.' Churchill took her magnifying glass from her handbag and examined it. 'Yes, it looks like a broken piece of stoneware, alright. Store it carefully in your handbag, Pembers. It's sharp and we may be able to get a fingerprint from it.' She glanced around her. 'We must be standing in the spot where the murder took place.'

Pemberley shuddered. 'What a horrible thought!'

'It's not nice, is it? Now, can we find any more pieces?'

Their search uncovered two more shards of the teapot, then Churchill caught sight of something shining in the sunlight.

'This is very interesting,' she said, picking it up and placing it in her palm. 'A button from a police uniform. It has a little coat of arms on it and the words Dorset Constabulary. What a find! It must have come off Chief Inspector Llewellyn-Dalrymple's jacket.'

'Or Inspector Kendall's jacket,' said Pemberley.

'That's a thought.'

'Or even Inspector Mappin's jacket.'

'Golly. Do you think it's possible? I think we need to pay him a visit.' She dropped the button into her handbag and fastened it securely. 'Even though he's supposed to have retired, I have a feeling we'll find him at the police station.'

Chapter Seven

As Churchill had predicted, Inspector Mappin was sitting behind his shiny walnut desk at Compton Poppleford police station.

'So much for retirement, eh Inspector?' she said.

'My retirement is postponed for the time being, Mrs Churchill. With a crime as serious as this, the investigation needs an experienced officer like me.'

'I see. And what does Inspector Kendall think about that?'

'Who's interested in what he thinks? He's as much use as a chocolate fireguard.'

'He cut his teeth in Salisbury.'

'He could have cut his teeth in John O'Groats for all I care. This murder investigation requires a senior officer with local knowledge and a nose for the truth.'

'Oh. And where are you going to find an officer like that?'

His face reddened. 'I was referring to myself, Mrs Churchill!'

She smiled. 'I know you were, Inspector. I was just making a little joke.'

'This is no time for jokes!'

'Very well. Are you missing a button?'

'I don't think so. Why?'

'Miss Pemberley and I found this at the scene of the crime.' Churchill took the button from her handbag and gave it to him.

Mappin picked up the button and examined it closely, turning it over between his fingers. 'Looks like a standard issue Dorset Constabulary button,' he said, frowning. 'And you found it at the scene, you say?'

Churchill nodded.

'You're not meddling in this investigation, are you?'

'No, Inspector. We're being helpful.'

He placed the button carefully on the desk. 'Well yes, I suppose this button is quite helpful. Where's it from?' He got to his feet and took off his jacket, turning it over and carefully examining the front. His brow furrowed. 'It's not from my jacket. All the buttons are here.' He tapped them one by one to check.

'And what about Inspector Kendall's jacket?' asked Churchill. 'Is it missing any buttons?'

'Not that I recall,' said Mappin. 'And besides, it couldn't have come from his jacket, he was buying an ice cream at the time of the murder.'

'So this means this button must have come from Chief Inspector Llewellyn-Dalrymple's jacket,' said Churchill. 'Unless there was another officer present that day who lost a button.'

Mappin put on his jacket again. 'Lots of uniformed officers were at the party and they probably all visited the refreshments tent. The button could be from any one of them.'

'If the button came off the chief inspector's uniform during the attack, then it's possible there was a physical struggle between him and his attacker,' said Churchill.

'But no one heard anything from the refreshments tent,' said Pemberley.

'It's a puzzle,' said Inspector Mappin. 'But I'll get to the bottom of it, don't you worry.'

'And what about the remains of the teapot, Inspector?' asked Churchill. 'Are they being examined for fingerprints?'

'Yes. The teapot remains are now in a specialist police department in Dorchester where the teapot is being reconstructed and expertly examined.'

'That sounds excellent,' said Churchill. She chose not to tell him about the shards she and Pemberley had discovered because she wanted to examine them herself.

'Not that you need to know any of this, Mrs Churchill,' continued Inspector Mappin. 'I'm in charge of the investigation, and I don't need anyone else meddling in it. That includes Inspector Kendall as well as you and Miss Pemberley.'

'Of course. And all this must be very upsetting for you, Inspector. After all, Chief Inspector Llewellyn-Dalrymple was your colleague.'

'Yes.' He sat back in his chair and gave a sad nod. 'Murder is a terrible crime. But the murder of a fellow officer... it's almost indescribable.'

'Very sad indeed. Were you friendly with him outside of your police work?'

'No. Not really. He was the rank above me, and he moved in different social circles.'

'Naturally. And it must feel odd for you working again when you were all prepared for retirement.'

'Yes. But I have a duty to find out who murdered my superior.'

'When we spoke to your wife yesterday, she told us how the chief inspector was forcing you to retire against your wishes and that you were close to despair about it.'

Inspector Mappin scratched his nose. 'My wife likes to exaggerate these things, but that's pretty much the long and the short of it.'

'And the sudden absence of Chief Inspector Llewellyn-Dalrymple means you're able to reprise your role.'

'I haven't really looked at it like that, but I suppose it does.'

'A complete outsider who doesn't know you at all, Inspector, might suggest that the death of your boss has allowed you to continue doing the career you love,' said Pemberley.

'Yes, I suppose a complete outsider could say that.'

'And the complete outsider might even be tempted to think you murdered your boss in order to continue doing the career you love.'

He scowled. 'Well, the complete outsider would be completely mistaken! And as you mentioned, Miss Pemberley, the complete outsider doesn't know me, so how could they possibly suggest such a thing?' He pointed a finger at her. 'Are you suggesting I could have carried out this crime?'

'No, absolutely not. I was merely trying to put myself in the shoes of a complete outsider,' said Pemberley.

'One could argue the murderer had something to gain from Chief Inspector Llewellyn-Dalrymple's death,' said Churchill. 'The facts suggest you had something to gain, Inspector. You've managed to put your retirement on hold and continue with your job.'

He glowered at her. 'If anyone thinks I murdered the

chief inspector to keep my job, then they need their head examining!'

'You can still retire,' said Churchill. 'You can hand the case over to Inspector Kendall and let him deal with it.'

'I don't want to. He's hopeless! I'm going to petition for him to be sent back to Salisbury.'

'Very well.'

'And you need to go back to your office now, ladies. I don't have time for any more cloaked accusations. You really do need to watch your step, you know.'

'Steps.'

'Steps? What do you mean?'

'There are two of us, Inspector, so step needs to be plural.'

'Just get out of my station.' He pointed at the door. 'Now.'

Churchill and Pemberley stepped back out into the sunshine. Oswald had waited patiently for them by the door and greeted them with an excited wag of his tail.

'That was a very satisfying sparring session with Inspector Mappin, wasn't it?' said Churchill. 'When his retirement was announced, I feared we would never cross swords again. But now it feels like old times again.'

'Do you think he murdered Chief Inspector Llewellyn-Dalrymple?' asked Pemberley.

Churchill gave this some thought. 'I'm not sure. He had a strong motive for getting rid of him, but could he have actually committed the crime? It's difficult to imagine it.'

'We need to consider all possibilities.'

'You're right, Pemberley, we do.' Churchill breathed in

The Teapot Killer

the warm spring air. 'Isn't it a lovely day? I fancy a little lunchtime stroll by the river. What do you say?'

'I'm afraid I can't. Miss Applethorn and I have already arranged to meet for a stroll by the river.'

'Oh. I see.' Churchill tried to ignore the sinking disappointment in her chest.

'In fact, I'm just off to meet her now.'

'Are you indeed? Well, have a nice time, Pemberley.'

'You too, Mrs Churchill. See you later.'

Churchill gave a sniff and went on her way. She felt determined to stroll by the river, even if she was going to do it alone.

Chapter Eight

The peaceful riverside scene soon lifted Churchill's spirits. Ducks and swans floated peacefully by, and elegant weeping willows dipped their fresh green foliage in the water. Churchill gave a little exclamation of delight when she caught a flash of blue—a kingfisher diving off a branch into the river.

As she continued along the path, she noticed two lanky figures and two dogs approaching her. Pemberley and Miss Applethorn had clearly decided to walk alongside the river in the opposite direction. The pair were so deeply engrossed in conversation that they didn't notice Churchill until she was almost upon them.

'Oh, hello, Mrs Churchill,' said Pemberley. 'Are you enjoying your walk?'

'Yes, I'm enjoying it enormously.' She smiled broadly to show she could have fun by herself.

'That's good,' said Pemberley. 'I'll see you back at the office.'

The two ladies resumed their conversation, and

Oswald paused briefly to sniff Churchill's legs before trotting after them.

The encounter had been disappointingly brief. She felt a pang of jealousy as their voices faded into the distance.

Back at the office, Churchill ate three slices of gingerbread cake before Pemberley and Oswald returned.

'Did you have a pleasant walk, Pemberley?'

'Yes. Miss Applethorn and I took a slightly longer route.'

Churchill glanced at the clock on the wall. 'Half past two. We really should get on with this afternoon's work.'

'Yes, we should. Shall I make some tea?'

'Oh, alright then.'

'I've been telling Miss Applethorn all about our detective work,' said Pemberley once the tea was made. 'She's very interested in it all.'

'Well, that's nice.'

'She's so interested, in fact, that she would like to join us.'

Churchill felt a pang of indignation. 'No, I'm afraid not, Pemberley. She has no detective experience whatsoever.'

'We had little detective experience when we set up the agency.'

'Actually, we did. I was married to a chief inspector for many years, and you worked for Atkins, who previously owned this detective agency. So between us, we had lots of experience, and we've proved ourselves with all the crimes we have solved. I'm afraid Miss Applethorn just wouldn't be suitable.'

'But she's very clever.'

'Being clever isn't enough. There are many skills one

needs to be a detective, and I'm afraid most people don't have them.'

'But she would be willing to learn. And she wouldn't expect us to pay her either. She says she's happy to do it in her free time when she's not working in the library.'

'We're a professional detective agency! This is no place for amateurs. And besides, we don't need a third person. We function perfectly well with just the two of us.'

'Oh, that's a terrible shame. Miss Applethorn will be desperately upset when I tell her that.'

'Well, I'm sorry to hear it, but we can't simply take an extra person on just because they like the idea of it. And besides, there's a waiting list.'

'Is there? Who else is on the list?'

'Mrs Thonnings. As you know, she's been badgering us to join the detective agency for a few years now. The only way of placating her is to tell her she's on the list. Perhaps you can tell that to Miss Applethorn too.'

Churchill picked up another slice of gingerbread cake from the plate on her desk and bit into it.

'And how long will she have to wait on the waiting list?' asked Pemberley.

'It's impossible to say. And if she isn't happy with that answer, then she's a very demanding friend.'

'Miss Applethorn is not demanding. She's a very easy-going friend.'

'Well, that's good to hear, Pemberley. But you'll have to tell her that for the time being, there is no vacancy. Now then, let's get on with examining those shards of teapot we found at the murder scene. Where's Atkins's fingerprint dusting kit?'

A short while later, the two ladies sat at Churchill's desk with the shards of teapot laid out on pieces of blotting paper and the fingerprint testing kit ready for use.

The Teapot Killer

Churchill selected a small brush with long, soft bristles, opened a tin of dark powder and dipped the brush into it. Then she dusted over a teapot shard with light, flitting movements.

'Can you see any fingerprints yet?' asked Pemberley.

'Nothing particularly clear. Let's try another shard.'

'The powder always makes me sneeze.'

'Well, make sure you do it on the other side of the office. I don't want you sneezing all over our scientific work. Oh darn it, I can't see a decent fingerprint on this one either.'

Churchill began to dust the third shard. Her heart lifted when she saw a clear fingerprint revealing itself.

'Look, Pembers! We have something!'

'How can you be sure it's not one of our fingerprints?'

'We'll take prints of ours, just to be certain. But we've handled these shards extremely carefully and I think it's paid off!'

Churchill took a piece of tape from the fingerprint kit and laid it over the fingerprint on the shard of teapot. Slowly and carefully, she lifted the tape again and stuck it to a piece of card. 'There! What a splendid specimen. I do believe you and I are looking at the fingerprint of Chief Inspector Llewellyn-Dalrymple's murderer, Pembers!'

'Golly.' She gave a shudder.

Churchill took an ink block and pad out of her desk drawer. 'Now then, let's take prints of our own fingers, just to be certain.'

'And of Oswald's paws.'

'Oswald's paws?'

'Yes. He doesn't like being left out.'

. . .

Pemberley made more tea and, a short while later, cards with Churchill and Pemberley's fingerprints and Oswald's paw prints were laid out on Churchill's desk.

She took out her magnifying glass and examined everything closely. 'I can say with certainty now, Pemberley, that the fingerprint on the teapot shard does not belong to you or me. Isn't that marvellous?'

'Or Oswald.'

'Or Oswald. So now we have to find the person this fingerprint matches to.'

'So we need to collect fingerprints from our suspects?' asked Pemberley.

'Yes.'

'How?'

'We just have to use our cunning.'

Footsteps sounded on the staircase beyond their office door.

'Oh no,' said Churchill. 'Who's this who's come to bother us?'

Chapter Nine

Mrs Thonnings stepped into the office. Her red hair, usually bouncy and curly, was flat. She slumped into a chair opposite Churchill, her expression weary.

'Oh dear, Mrs Thonnings. You don't look your best today, if you don't mind me saying so.'

'I'm not. I hardly slept last night.'

'The shock of the murder of Chief Inspector Llewellyn-Dalrymple?'

'Yes, that is quite shocking. But I also can't stop thinking about the simnel cake.'

'I'm sure it's just a coincidence that Mrs Honeypear's grandmother's recipe is very similar to yours, Mrs Thonnings.'

'No, it isn't. I could even taste the secret ingredient!'

'Is it possible that Mrs Honeypear's grandmother also thought of the same secret ingredient?'

'No! I refuse to believe it. And when I got home yesterday, I checked to see if my simnel cake recipe was still there.'

'And was it?' asked Churchill.

'Yes.'

'Oh. So the recipe hasn't been stolen.'

'No, but it wasn't where I left it.'

'Where did you leave it?'

'I think it's better if you and Miss Pemberley come with me to my cottage. It will make more sense that way.'

'Very well.'

Mrs Thonnings lived in a cosy little cottage close to her haberdashery shop. Inside, a Welsh dresser displayed blue-and-white china and wooden beams stretched across the low ceiling. A tabby cat dozed in an armchair covered in faded chintz.

'I'll show you where I keep all the secret family recipes,' said Mrs Thonnings, opening a cupboard in the bottom of the dresser. She pulled out a battered wicker sewing basket and set it on a sturdy oak table. She opened it to reveal rolls of thread, a pincushion and colourful scraps of fabric and ribbon.

'It looks like a box of sewing supplies to me, Mrs Thonnings.'

'That's what it's supposed to look like. But if you lift these out, then you'll find the recipes.'

Churchill and Pemberley watched as she pulled out the sewing supplies and dropped them onto the table.

'Do you see? At the bottom are my secret family recipes.'

Churchill peered into the basket at the tatty pieces of paper. 'Yes, I see.'

'The simnel cake recipe is on top,' said Mrs Thonnings. She pulled it out and showed it to them. It was hand-written in faded ink and had a few grease marks and spatters on it. 'But I didn't leave it on top. I've since made the rhubarb crumble and the jam tarts. I haven't made the simnel cake for almost a year, so there's no reason why it should be on top of the other recipes.'

'Isn't it possible that you shuffled the recipes around when you last opened this basket?' asked Pemberley.

'No. I never shuffle my recipes around. Someone has got into this sewing basket, found the simnel cake recipe, copied it down and put it back in its not quite proper place.'

Churchill scratched her chin. The idea seemed a little far-fetched to her, but Mrs Thonnings seemed quite certain about it. 'So who's visited your cottage recently, Mrs Thonnings? Has Mrs Honeypear been here?'

'No. Mrs Honeypear has never been here.'

'So that means she couldn't have got to the recipe and copied it down.'

'No. Someone must have done it for her. Either she asked them to do it, or they were an opportunist who sold it to her.'

'Who on earth would bother to do that?'

Mrs Thonnings shrugged. 'I don't know. That's what you and Miss Pemberley have to find out, Mrs Churchill.'

'You want us to investigate this?'

'Absolutely. I can't have my family's secret simnel cake recipe spread about the village. And I certainly don't want Mrs Honeypear baking it and getting all the credit for it at retirement parties.'

Churchill sighed. 'Well, I suppose you'd better give us a list of the people who've visited your home recently, Mrs Thonnings.'

'I haven't had many visitors other than the Compton Poppleford Ladies' Sewing Circle.'

'How would a member of the Ladies' Sewing Circle have got into your sewing basket without you noticing?'

'I don't know. But it could have been while we were all in the front room having tea and biscuits. Someone could have sneaked in here, got into my sewing basket, and copied down my grandmother's recipe for simnel cake.'

'And did you notice anyone missing while you were having tea?'

'People were coming and going. A few went off for a comfort break, that sort of thing. Or what I assumed was a comfort break, anyway. For all I know, they were copying down my simnel cake recipe.'

'How would anyone know where it is?'

'I don't know.' Mrs Thonnings shrugged again. 'That's the mystery.'

'How many ladies from the Sewing Circle were here that day?' asked Churchill.

'Eighteen.'

'Goodness. Eighteen people? How did they all fit in here?'

'We manage one way or another.'

Churchill took her notebook and pen out of her handbag. 'I suppose we'd better get a list of names, then.'

'Of course. There's Mrs Higginbath.'

'Really? You let her into your home?'

'Yes, Mrs Higginbath enjoys sewing. I don't know what you've got against her, Mrs Churchill.'

'I've only got something against her because she's got something against me.' Churchill wrote down her name. 'And who else?'

'Well, there's Mrs Harris. She's very keen on sewing. She's currently making a little coat for her dog.'

'How lovely,' said Pemberley. 'I wish I was skilled enough at needlework to make a little coat for Oswald.'

The Teapot Killer

'You can always learn, Miss Pemberley,' said Mrs Thonnings. 'If you join the Ladies' Sewing Circle, then we can help you.'

'Well, there's an idea,' said Pemberley. 'I always thought I would hate sewing, but I'm tempted if it means Oswald can have a little jacket. In fact, I could ask Miss Applethorn if she would like to come too, and she could make a matching coat for Whisker. The two little dogs would look adorable in them!'

'I'm sure they would,' said Churchill, growing impatient.

'Miss Applethorn is already a member of the Ladies' Sewing Circle,' said Mrs Thonnings.

'Is she?' said Pemberley, excitedly. 'Then I must join!'

'We're here to investigate the simnel cake recipe,' said Churchill. She turned back to Mrs Thonnings. 'Now, tell me the rest of the names.'

Churchill surveyed her list once she'd written down all eighteen names. 'Which of these ladies are friendly with Mrs Honeypear?'

'I don't know,' said Mrs Thonnings.

Churchill sighed. 'I was hoping you'd be a little more helpful than that.'

'Some of them are probably friends with her, some of them probably know her reasonably well but not enormously well, and I imagine some people don't know her at all.'

'I see. That's useful, Mrs Thonnings.'

A pause followed, then Mrs Thonnings lowered her voice. 'There's one other person who's visited my cottage recently,' she said. 'Quite a lot, in fact.'

'And who's that?'

'Well, I'm a little reluctant to say because our relationship is still in its early days.'

'Is it a new man friend of yours, Mrs Thonnings?'

Her face coloured. 'Well, since you put it like that, yes. I suppose he is my new man friend.'

'And who is he?'

'Mr Greystone, the undertaker.'

Churchill startled at this. 'The undertaker?'

'Yes. He's very handsome, and we like to play cards together.'

'I see. Mr Greystone, the undertaker. Well, let's write his name down as well. Does he know Mrs Honeypear?'

'No.'

'Right.'

'I'm sorry, Mrs Churchill. You're probably already very busy investigating Chief Inspector Llewellyn-Dalrymple's murder, aren't you? I hate to burden you with this, but it really is bothering me.'

'That's fine, Mrs Thonnings.' Churchill folded her notebook shut and put it back in her handbag.

'Talking of murder, I had an interesting conversation with Mrs Harris in the greengrocer's this morning,' said Mrs Thonnings. 'We were discussing the terrible events at Inspector Mappin's retirement party, and she says her friend Mrs Runcey saw Mrs Beanfork hit Chief Inspector Llewellyn-Dalrymple with her handbag.'

'Goodness, really? Who's Mrs Beanfork?'

'She's the lady with all the cats who lives up near the farm and has the wayward son.'

'I see. What does her son get up to?'

'He's just come out of prison where he spent three years for robbing Mr Gilding's jeweller's shop.'

'I see. And his mother hit the chief inspector with her handbag at the retirement party? Have you any idea why?'

Mrs Thonnings shook her head. 'No. But I could ask Mrs Harris to ask Mrs Runcey.'

'Don't worry, Miss Pemberley and I can ask Mrs Beanfork ourselves. Thank you for the information, Mrs Thonnings. Mrs Beanfork clearly had a gripe with Llewellyn-Dalrymple, and we need to find out what it was.'

Chapter Ten

'THE BAKERY IS OFFERING FOUR CHOCOLATE ECLAIRS FOR the price of three,' said Pemberley when she arrived at the office the following morning. 'So I got six.'

'Why not eight?' asked Churchill.

'Because it was four for the price of three.'

'Yes. So you could have got eight for the price of six.'

'No, it was only four for the price of three.'

Churchill sighed. 'Oh, never mind, Pembers. At least we have three each, which is just what we need with our busy day ahead of us. We've got to pay Mrs Beanfork a visit. What do you know about her?'

'She has a lot of cats and a wayward son.'

'Yes, that's what Mrs Thonnings told us yesterday. Anything else?'

'No. That's all I know. I'll make some tea.'

'Excellent. And I'll make a start on our incident board.'

It was a ritual which Churchill enjoyed whenever she was working on a new case. Using photographs, notes, and pieces of string, she liked to pin all the information on a map of Compton Poppleford on the wall.

The Teapot Killer

She stood back and admired her handiwork as Pemberley returned with the tea.

'We have two suspects so far,' said Churchill. 'Mrs Honeypear because she was the person who discovered the murder which had been carried out in her refreshments tent with her teapot. And Inspector Mappin because he was upset that Chief Inspector Llewellyn-Dalrymple was forcing him to retire.'

'And we found a police officer's button at the scene which could belong to him. Although he denies it.'

'True.'

'And we have a fingerprint.'

'Yes! The sooner we can get Mrs Honeypear and Inspector Mappin's fingerprints, the better.'

'And Mrs Beanfork seems suspicious too.'

'That's right, she does! All this business of hitting the chief inspector with her handbag. Perhaps she was disappointed the handbag wasn't heavy enough and progressed to the teapot? We need answers.'

They were interrupted by footsteps on the staircase.

'I hope that's not Mrs Thonnings again,' said Churchill. 'I'm too busy to investigate simnel cake recipes.'

A knock sounded at the door, then sharp-featured Inspector Kendall strode in. He took off his cap, hung it on the hat stand, and stood in the centre of the office with his hands on his hips.

'So this is the detective agency I've heard all about.' He surveyed the room. 'You have a nice little setup here, ladies.'

Churchill bristled. She didn't need the new inspector telling her what he thought of her detective agency. 'How can we help you?' she asked coldly.

'I thought I'd visit you for a little chat.'

'About what?' She didn't feel inclined to offer him a seat, a cup of tea, or an eclair.

'Just a little chat about the village in general, really. I'm interested in the sorts of characters you have here.' He grabbed a chair, span it round and sat on it back-to-front with his legs either side.

Churchill wrinkled her nose and retreated to the seat behind her desk.

'You two ladies must know the local characters quite well,' said the inspector.

'Not enormously well,' replied Churchill. 'I arrived here from London just a few years ago.'

'London? So you've experienced city life, like me.'

'You're from Salisbury, Inspector. It's hardly comparable to the mean streets of London.'

'It's a city. It has a cathedral.'

'So I've heard.'

'Anyway, back to the local characters. As I'm new to the area, I don't know many of them. So I was hoping you could point me in the right direction.'

'Suggest people who we think might have murdered Chief Inspector Llewellyn-Dalrymple?'

'Absolutely. You understand me completely, Mrs Churchill. I've heard that you and Miss Pemberley crack most of the cases in this village. Dozy-faced Mappin can't take credit for any of them.'

Churchill felt reluctant to share any information with him. 'We don't have an opinion on this latest murder because it's very high-profile and out of our league. A senior member of the force was murdered, and the investigation requires a robust team from the Dorset Constabulary.'

'I couldn't agree with you more, and I'm taking the lead in this complex investigation. It's in good hands. But I need to know what the locals are saying. Who had it in for Llewellyn-Dalrymple?'

'I suggest you consult your colleague, Inspector Mappin,' said Churchill. 'He's spent his entire policing career in this village, so you'll have to bother him with your questions, not us. We're very busy with other business.'

Inspector Kendall rubbed his chin. 'Yes, but unfortunately Mappin and I don't get along too well.'

'You'll have to sort that out between you,' said Churchill. 'If you hadn't marched into this village and attempted to steal his job, then I'm sure you would get on a little better.'

'The decision to move me here was made high up in the chain. On the orders of Superintendent Trowelbank, no less. Above Llewellyn-Dalrymple's head. The Superintendent had a quiet word with me because he was disappointed with how Compton Poppleford was being policed. He then had a word with Llewellyn-Dalrymple, and he made it happen.' He clicked his fingers and winked at the same time.

Churchill felt her toes curl.

'Trowelbank was very impressed with me at Salisbury,' continued the inspector. 'He put his hand on my shoulder and said, "Kendall, this is a sideways move for the time being, but I need you in Compton Poppleford to sort out those country bumpkins. The murder rate is through the roof and Mappin is resting on his laurels. And besides, if you stay here in Salisbury then you'll be offered my job before you know it and I'll be out on my ear."' Inspector Kendall slapped his thigh and laughed. 'He actually said that!'

Churchill stared at him and allowed an uncomfortable silence to build.

Inspector Kendall cleared his throat and scratched the

back of his head. 'So yes… anyway. I must say I'm a little disappointed with my visit here today. I'd heard a lot about your detective skills, and I was hoping you'd be more helpful.'

'Well, I'm sorry you're disappointed, Inspector, but you'll need to do some good old-fashioned legwork, I'm afraid. Detective work is a difficult business.'

He got up from the chair and put on his cap. Then he caught sight of the incident board. Churchill's heart sank as he strolled over to it. 'Look at this! So you are looking into the case after all!'

'No. That's an investigation into a stolen cake recipe.'

'And Mappin is a suspect?'

'Yes.'

The inspector threw back his head and laughed. 'No wonder top brass wanted him out! Oh dear, that's the funniest thing I've heard all day.' He wiped a tear of mirth from his eye. 'I'll see you around, ladies.'

Churchill felt her shoulders relax once he'd left.

'I don't like that man,' said Pemberley, sullenly.

'Me neither. He has a high opinion of himself, doesn't he? And he's absolutely clueless too. I thought Mappin was hapless, but Kendall really has no idea whatsoever. Perhaps I was rather rude to him just now, but I got the impression that he wanted us to do his work for him.'

'I got that impression too,' said Pemberley. 'And I'm confused about who's officially investigating the case. Is it him? Or is it Inspector Mappin, even though he's supposed to have retired?'

Churchill shook her head. 'It's all a mess, Pemberley. And it must be a terrible worry for Mrs Llewellyn-Dalrymple. So I think it's best that you and I tackle this case and help her get justice.'

'I feel very sorry for her that her husband died. But I

don't like her very much,' said Pemberley. 'I found her quite unfriendly at the retirement party.'

'I don't disagree with you, Pembers. No one deserves to have their husband murdered, but she's not an easy person to feel sympathy for. I must admit, I didn't really like Llewellyn-Dalrymple much either. But that's not the reason we do these things, is it? We do these things because it is right.'

'And we also do these things because whoever is brazen enough to murder Chief Inspector Llewellyn-Dalrymple with a giant teapot could do it again.'

Churchill shivered. 'You're absolutely right, Pemberley! They should be locked up as soon as possible. And with the local constabulary in chaos, it's down to you and me to work it out.'

Chapter Eleven

It was a long walk to Mrs Beanfork's home on the edge of the village. The rambling, whitewashed cottage was perched at the top of a steep farm track.

Pemberley picked up Oswald when Churchill knocked at the crooked oak door. 'I need to protect him from the cats,' she explained.

A pear-shaped lady with frizzy grey hair and horn-rimmed spectacles answered the door. 'Yes?'

Churchill introduced herself and Pemberley. 'We're investigating the murder of Chief Inspector Llewellyn-Dalrymple,' she added.

'Why?'

'Because the police are rather disorganised at the moment and we think our detective agency is better placed to investigate what happened.'

Mrs Beanfork folded her arms. 'I'm not sure why you're bothering.'

'We hear you had an encounter with the chief inspector at the retirement party. Would you mind telling us about it?'

'There's nothing much to say. But I can't leave you hanging about on my doorstep, so you'd better come in.'

A tortoiseshell cat, a black and white cat, and a tabby accompanied them as they followed Mrs Beanfork to the parlour. Oswald cowered in Pemberley's arms.

In the parlour, every seat was occupied.

'Just move a cat and sit down,' said Mrs Beanfork, scooping up a ginger cat from an armchair.

Churchill and Pemberley hesitated. 'I don't really like moving cats,' said Churchill. 'Especially when they look so rested.'

'They do it on purpose so you don't move them,' said Mrs Beanfork. 'They're very sneaky like that.'

'I'm fine standing up,' said Churchill.

'Oh, what nonsense. Let's see if we can find somewhere to sit in the kitchen.'

Fortunately, the rickety wooden chairs in the kitchen were empty. As soon as Churchill sat on one, she realised why the cats avoided it. She hoped they could get through their conversation with Mrs Beanfork before her posterior went numb.

'Tea?'

'Yes, please.'

Mrs Beanfork made herself busy at the hearth and Churchill wondered if she was going to admit she'd hit Chief Inspector Llewellyn-Dalrymple with her handbag. 'Did you speak to the chief inspector at the retirement party?' she asked.

'Oh yes. As soon as I saw him, I was seized with anger. I couldn't help myself. I went up to him and hit him with my handbag.'

'I see,' said Churchill nonchalantly, pretending this was normal behaviour.

'Unfortunately, it was my brown handbag which is

fairly lightweight. I wish I'd had my burgundy one with me as that has some sharp corners on it.'

Churchill winced. 'Oh.'

'I didn't see him again after that. And the next thing I heard, he was dead.'

'Would you mind telling us why you attacked the chief inspector?'

'I didn't attack him,' replied Mrs Beanfork, carrying a teapot over to the table. 'I hit him with my handbag.'

'Why?'

She put her hands on her wide hips. 'Because he locked my son, Fred, up for three years!'

'Oh dear! I'm sorry to hear it. What was his reason?'

'He claimed Fred robbed Mr Gilding's jeweller's shop.'

'Presumably there was a trial?'

'Yes, there was. And Llewellyn-Dalrymple spoke so convincingly during the trial that the jury convicted my son, and he was sentenced. A completely innocent young man! He had to spend three years in Dorchester prison.'

'And he was innocent, you say?'

Mrs Beanfork gave a fierce nod. 'Absolutely. Wrongly convicted because Chief Inspector Llewellyn-Dalrymple wanted to make sure someone was imprisoned for the crime.'

'And how is your son now?'

'Well, he's just come out. He's served his time—not that he should ever have been in there in the first place—and now he's working for Farmer Drumhead. Three years of his life have gone down the drain and all because of Llewellyn-Dalrymple.'

'So it's fair to say, then, that you and your son Fred bore some resentment towards the chief inspector?'

'Oh yes! Lots of resentment.' She took a biscuit jar from the dresser and plonked it on the table. 'I'm still extremely angry about it now, even though he's dead. Isn't it strange? Even when someone's dead, you can still be angry with them.'

'Well, yes, that can happen sometimes. Did you speak to Chief Inspector Llewellyn-Dalrymple about your son's supposed wrongful conviction?'

'There's nothing supposed about it, Mrs Churchill—it was a wrongful conviction. His solicitor said so.' She poured out the tea. 'I spoke to Llewellyn-Dalrymple practically every week about it, but he wouldn't listen. He wasn't interested. He just dismissed me with a wave of his hand. And when I saw him at Inspector Mappin's retirement party, the anger and the hatred bubbled up all over again.' She accidentally slopped some tea into Churchill's saucer. 'Oops, sorry about that. Do you mind tipping it into your cup? Anyway, I don't regret hitting him with my handbag. I don't think it hurt him too much, and it made me feel better.'

'And it seems someone else was angry with him that day because they fatally injured him with an oversized teapot,' said Pemberley.

Mrs Beanfork sat at the table and gave a firm nod. 'And I wasn't sorry when I heard about it, either.'

'Were you tempted at any time to knock him out with that teapot?' asked Churchill.

'I wish I'd thought of it! But someone braver and cleverer than me did it instead.'

'Have you any idea who that brave, clever person might be?'

Mrs Beanfork shook her head. 'No idea whatsoever.'

Churchill took a sip of tea and looked hopefully at the biscuit jar which still had its lid on. Mrs Beanfork missed the hint. 'What were you doing when the Morris dancers were dancing?' she asked.

'Fred and I were watching them, of course.'

'Can anyone vouch for that?'

'Why would someone need to vouch for it?'

'Oh, you know what it's like with these investigations, Mrs Beanfork—it's quite usual for someone else to back you up when you say you were in a certain place at a certain time.'

'Well, in which case I think everybody there would have seen us watching the Morris dancers. You were probably there as well, weren't you?'

'Yes, I was there.'

'I remember seeing you there, Mrs Churchill. You're a difficult lady to miss with your erm…' Mrs Beanfork eyed her large frame. 'Upright posture.'

'I see.'

'And no one can miss lanky Miss Pemberley with her unkempt hair and faded cardigans.'

Churchill and Pemberley exchanged a wounded glance. 'Would it be possible to have a biscuit?' Churchill asked. 'I worked up quite an appetite walking up here.'

'Oh, of course!' Mrs Beanfork took the lid off the biscuit jar and placed some biscuits on a plate. 'Do you like custard creams?'

Churchill's mouth watered. 'I love custard creams.' As she bit into the biscuit, she realised she had to get a fingerprint from Mrs Beanfork. 'Can I trouble you for a glass of water as well?' she asked.

'Water?'

'Yes.'

'To drink?'

'Yes.'

'But you have tea, Mrs Churchill.'

'I know. I apologise for being so demanding.' She gave

The Teapot Killer

a broad smile and Mrs Beanfork got up from the table to fetch some water from the water pump.

'I can't believe she described my hair as unkempt!' whispered Pemberley. 'What about the state of her hair? I don't think it's seen a comb for several years.'

'Never mind that, Pembers. I think she's a strong murder suspect, don't you? Dissatisfied with the handbag attack, she progressed to the teapot. And she's got thick forearms too. I think she had the strength to wield it.'

Mrs Beanfork returned and placed the glass of water on the table. 'There you are, Mrs Churchill. Now, is there anything else I can help with?'

'We'd like to speak to Fred, too. He works for Farmer Drumhead, you say?'

'Yes. Farmer Drumhead has been very kind to him. No one wants to employ a young man who's been in prison for three years, but Farmer Drumhead always believed Fred was innocent.'

'Well, that's interesting to hear,' said Churchill. 'I rent my cottage from Farmer Drumhead and have always held him in high regard. It's good to know that he has a high opinion of your son.' She drained her glass of water.

'I don't think there's any use in speaking to Fred though, he'll only tell you what I've just told you.'

'We like to speak to as many people as possible.'

Mrs Beanfork sighed. 'I've already told you it's a waste of your time. The wicked chief inspector is dead and I don't think you'll find too many people who are upset about it.' She got to her feet. 'I'll show you out.'

Five cats accompanied them to the door, and Oswald remained in Pemberley's arms.

'Before you go, Mrs Churchill, can I trouble you for the return of my glass?'

'Your glass?'

'Yes. The one I served water to you in. I saw you put it in your handbag.'

Churchill's heart sank. She thought she'd done it without being noticed. She forced a laugh. 'Did I? Oh, how silly of me.' She opened her handbag, reluctantly removed the glass, and handed it back to Mrs Beanfork. 'It's a habit of mine, you see. I often take a glass with me when I leave home. Just in case I need some water from a water fountain and…' She trailed off, realising her explanation was going nowhere. 'Anyway. Thank you for the tea and custard creams, Mrs Beanfork.'

Chapter Twelve

CHURCHILL AND PEMBERLEY MADE THEIR WAY TOWARDS Farmer Drumhead's hilltop farm. Oswald trotted merrily ahead of them, sniffing the hedgerow and seeming relieved to have escaped the cottage of cats.

'Gosh, what a lot of walking we're doing today,' said Churchill. 'It's just as well I've got my stout walking shoes on. And isn't it annoying how cat hair clings to Harris tweed?' She paused to brush the strands of fur from her skirt. 'I'm going to have to give this a good old going over with the clothes brush this evening.'

'It's a shame you didn't get away with the glass,' said Pemberley.

'Yes, it's an enormous shame. Mrs Beanfork is more eagled-eyed than I gave her credit for. She's a likely murderer, isn't she?'

'But if she's the murderer, then why would she admit to hitting Llewellyn-Dalrymple with her handbag? Surely she would want to deny she had anything against him.'

'She probably knew there were witnesses,' said Churchill.

'Yes, I suppose so. And maybe she's admitting to the lesser misdemeanour hoping she'll therefore be ruled out of the more serious one.'

'Goodness me, Pemberley, that's clever thinking! Nonetheless, she's on our list of suspects for now because she has a strong motive. It'll be interesting to see what young Fred Beanfork has to say for himself, won't it? Do you think he's innocent of the jewellery shop robbery?'

'I've always heard him described as wayward,' said Pemberley. 'But perhaps the description stuck after the robbery.'

'Or the supposed robbery. According to Fred Beanfork's mother, he wasn't responsible.'

'I can imagine a mother not wanting to admit her son is capable of such a thing.'

'I agree, Pemberley.'

They found Fred Beanfork repairing a fence by the farm track. He was pear-shaped, like his mother, and had fair, frizzy hair. A spindly cigarette hung from his lower lip.

'We've just been speaking to your mother,' said Churchill after she'd introduced herself to him. 'And we understand the pair of you had a grievance against Chief Inspector Llewellyn-Dalrymple.'

He squinted at them in the sunlight. 'Yeah, I didn't like him.'

'Because he sent you to prison?'

'Yeah. He told everyone I robbed Gilding's Jewellers when I did nothing of the sort.' Oswald sniffed his legs, and he gave the dog a pat.

'So you spent three years in prison when you were completely innocent?' said Churchill.

'Yeah. The trouble is, the only person who believes me

is my ma. Everyone else thinks I did it, and that's all because of LD.'

'LD?'

'Llewellyn-Dalrymple. I can't be bothered to say his name, it's too long.'

'Fair enough. Why do you think he was so determined to make sure you went to prison?'

'He just wanted to collar someone for it, didn't he? He didn't care who it was. He just wanted people to think he was good at solving crimes. But he wasn't. He was rubbish.'

'So what were you doing when Gilding's Jewellery shop was robbed?'

'I was fishing with my friend, Trotter.'

'So presumably Trotter provided you with an alibi?'

'Yeah. But LD didn't believe him because Trotter once lied about stealing apples from Colonel Slingsby's orchard.'

'Oh, I see. And one small lie led Chief Inspector Llewellyn-Dalrymple to believe your friend Trotter was an unreliable alibi. And he accused you of lying, too.'

'Yeah. He didn't believe either of us. And then I got locked up for three years.'

'Well, it's fortunate that Farmer Drumhead has given you employment here now. Hopefully, you can show everyone what an honest, hard-working young man you are.'

'Yeah. It's a shame though. I could have already been working here for three years by now if I hadn't been in jail.'

'Absolutely. What was taken during the robbery at the jeweller's?'

He shrugged. 'Jewellery, I suppose.'

'Was it ever recovered?'

'Don't know. Don't think so. That was another thing. If

they'd found the jewellery in my house, then that would've been proof I'd done it. But they didn't, because I didn't do the robbery.'

'Deary me, it doesn't sound like it was a thorough investigation. Did you speak to Chief Inspector Llewellyn-Dalrymple at Inspector Mappin's retirement party?'

'No. Never wanted nothing to do with him again. So I was happy when I heard he was dead.'

'You must have been quite tempted to hit him over the head with a teapot yourself.'

'Thought didn't even cross my mind. My ma gets angry about it still. From what I hear, she had a word or two with him at the party. But I wasn't interested. I just wanted to stay out of his way.' He pulled the limp cigarette end from his lip and tossed it onto the ground.

'You weren't tempted to wreak your revenge?'

'No point. Too late for that now, isn't it? I can't get the three years back. And I made some good friends in prison.'

'Well, that's a positive way of looking at it.'

'I like to think so.' He picked up his mallet and pulled out a nail from a pocket on his tool belt. 'I'd better get on.'

'Of course. Thank you for speaking to us, Mr Beanfork.'

Churchill stooped down, pretending to scratch her ankle. Then she surreptitiously picked up the discarded cigarette end and secreted it in her pocket.

Chapter Thirteen

Churchill and Pemberley updated their incident board when they returned to their office.

'It seems odd making Mrs Beanfork and her son suspects,' said Churchill. 'I thought the pair of them spoke quite honestly.'

'They could be good actors,' suggested Pemberley.

'Yes, that's true. Isn't human nature a funny thing? We want to trust people are telling us the truth and yet so many of them can be scheming liars. Oh well. We have four suspects now and I hope our list doesn't grow much bigger, otherwise we're going to have a lot of work on our hands.'

'Miss Applethorn is happy to help us, Mrs Churchill.'

'We don't need Miss Applethorn's help.'

'But—'

'No buts, Pemberley. Now I need to see if I can get a fingerprint from Fred Beanfork's cigarette end.' Churchill carefully retrieved it from her pocket.

'Ugh! You picked it up?'

'I had to. I'm afraid detective work can get rather

grubby at times.' Churchill placed the cigarette end on her desk and wrinkled her nose. 'I don't have high hopes about this, Pembers. It's going to be extremely difficult to get a fingerprint from a soggy, crumpled piece of cigarette.'

'I wouldn't bother,' said Pemberley. 'I wouldn't want to be within three yards of that grotty thing.'

'Sometimes detective work requires a strong stomach. In situations like this, one merely has to get the task done.'

Churchill fetched the fingerprint testing kit and got to work. Pemberley made some tea while she lightly dusted the cigarette end to reveal an elusive fingerprint. It wasn't long before she realised her efforts were in vain.

'Oh dear.' She sat back in her chair as Pemberley placed a cup of tea on her desk. 'Thank you, Pembers. I need that. It seems my attempts to obtain fingerprints from the Beanfork family have failed. But never mind. After we've drunk our tea, let's have a word with Mr Gilding the jeweller. I want to learn more about the robbery.'

Gilding's Jewellers had a smart, green polished shopfront and sparkling jewellery neatly arranged in the window.

'Look at that, Pembers!' Churchill peered in through the window. 'It's like Aladdin's Cave. And very tempting to a criminal, I should think. I'm surprised Gilding doesn't get burgled more often.'

A little bell rang on the door as they stepped inside. Churchill's feet sank into the soft carpet, and she felt dazzled by the twinkling displays in shiny glass cabinets.

Mr Gilding was a small, round, softly spoken man in a well-tailored suit. 'Good afternoon, ladies. How may I help you?'

Churchill introduced them both. 'We're interested to

learn more about the robbery you had here a few years ago, Mr Gilding.'

His brow furrowed. 'Oh, that. I don't like to think about it too much.'

'Would you mind thinking about it just briefly to help us with our investigation?'

'If you insist. What investigation?'

'We understand the recently deceased Chief Inspector Llewellyn-Dalrymple ensured that young Fred Beanfork was prosecuted for the robbery.'

'Yes, that's right. He got three years for it. And he's just been released after serving his time, I understand.'

'Young Beanfork maintains his innocence.'

'Well, he would do, wouldn't he? The criminal class always maintain their innocence.'

'So you believe Fred Beanfork was the robber?'

'Yes. That's what the police told me, anyway. I didn't really recognise him at the time because he had a stocking over his head with little holes cut in it so he could see. And then he had a hole for his mouth…' He shuddered. 'It was all quite creepy, really.'

'So you couldn't be completely certain that it was Fred Beanfork?'

'Well it was him, but I didn't know it at the time. I remember he had blue eyes.'

'And he was armed?'

'He had a large spade, and he threatened to hit me with it. I didn't want to hand over my jewels, of course, but I was very worried about being injured. And I reasoned I could claim back the value of the stolen goods on my insurance. So I didn't stand up to him much, I just let him get on with it.' He gave a sad sniff. 'It was rather cowardly of me, really.'

'It wasn't cowardly of you at all, Mr Gilding! You must have been very frightened.'

'I was.' He sniffed again.

'Fred Beanfork maintains he had an alibi for the time of the robbery.'

'Yes, I remember him saying so in court. Some young tearaway whose name I forget now. But obviously, he wasn't a reliable alibi, so no one paid any attention to that.'

'But could there have been a possibility the alibi was telling the truth?'

'I suppose there was a possibility. But the court found Fred Beanfork had committed the crime and so he was punished accordingly.'

'Who arrested Fred Beanfork?'

'The police.'

'Chief Inspector Llewellyn-Dalrymple, by any chance?'

'Yes. He was the one in charge. He called in here one day and told me they'd made an arrest, and I was very happy about it. They didn't recover the jewels, though. These criminals pass them on to someone else pretty quickly, don't they? They're not foolish. Anyway, they got him, and he's served his time, and that's all there is to it.'

'But do you think there's a possibility it could have been someone else who robbed you that day?'

He tapped his finger on his lips as he gave this some thought. 'I suppose it could have been someone else because I didn't see his face. And now that I think about it some more, there was someone I thought it was when he first strolled into the shop.'

Churchill leaned in closer. 'Who did you think it was, Mr Gilding?'

'That chap in the village who's a bit dodgy. Mr Letcher.'

The Teapot Killer

Pemberley gasped. 'Of course! I can imagine him doing something like that.'

'Who's Mr Letcher?' asked Churchill, feeling that she was missing something.

'He's a shifty local character,' said Pemberley. 'There are always rumours about him getting up to no good, but for some reason, he never seems to get punished.'

'Well, what sort of thing does he get up to?'

'Stealing things, robbing places, defrauding people. He's that sort of person. He runs Letcher's Garage and people often say the cars he sells there are stolen.'

'Gosh, he doesn't sound very pleasant.'

'He's not,' said Mr Gilding. 'And when the robber first stepped into the shop, Letcher did come to mind. But after that, I stopped thinking about who it was and tried to ensure I didn't get hit by his spade.'

'I'm not surprised,' said Churchill.

'He held out a little sack for me to put jewellery into, and he kept glancing around as if worried someone else might come in. It was all very quick, he was here for less than a minute.'

'So you saw the masked robber for less than a minute, yet Chief Inspector Llewellyn-Dalrymple managed to persuade everyone that he was Fred Beanfork,' said Churchill.

'Yes. I never doubted the chief inspector's judgement, of course—he was an extremely experienced police officer. He knew what he was doing, and I was happy that they caught the man.'

'Thank you, Mr Gilding. You've been very helpful.'

'Have I? I don't see how.'

'Trust me, you have.'

Chapter Fourteen

'Let's make our way to Letcher's Garage,' said Churchill once they'd left the jeweller's and were walking down the high street.

'Must we?' Pemberley shuddered. 'He's a horrible man.'

'But we have to speak to him, don't we? Mr Gilding seems to think it was him who robbed his jeweller's shop instead of Fred Beanfork.'

'But we can't possibly ask Letcher about that, Mrs Churchill! He'll be furious. And he's scary enough even when he's friendly.'

'Oh now, Pemberley. I'm sure there's nothing to be scared of. We're just two old ladies. He's not going to harm us, is he? We pose no threat to him whatsoever.'

'We do if we ask him about robbing jeweller's shops. He might even... oh, I don't even want to think about what he might do, Mrs Churchill. That man has a bad reputation.'

'Sometimes an investigation requires us to speak to

someone unpleasant. There are no two ways about it. Come along. These things are never as bad as you think they're going to be. Now remind me where Letcher's Garage is. I know I've passed it a few times, and it's a scruffy-looking place. I just can't remember exactly where it is.'

'It's on the South Bungerly Road. Opposite Greystone's funeral parlour.'

'Mrs Thonnings's Greystone?'

'Yes. Her man friend.'

Letcher's Garage was a sprawling business with several large sheds, a tumbledown kiosk and two petrol pumps. An adjacent yard had a handful of cars for sale and sun-faded signs saying, "Luxury Motorcars" and "Best Prices in Dorset".

Churchill and Pemberley approached one of the sheds where a door stood open. The sound of clanking tools and whistling came from within.

'Hello?' called out Churchill.

The whistling stopped. Then a broad man in oil-stained overalls stepped out. He had a mop of grey hair, narrow blue eyes, and was wiping his hands on a filthy rag.

'Hello, ladies. After a new motorcar? I've had some new ones in this week. There's a nice little Baby Austin, just twenty-four thousand miles on the clock. Or if you're after something more sophisticated, I've got a Singer Nine which only came in yesterday. A lovely motor car and it's going for a song. It won't be here long. I reckon I'll have sold it by the end of tomorrow, so you ladies have arrived at the perfect time.'

'Are you Mr Letcher?' asked Churchill.

'That's right. The proprietor of this fine establishment. I'll have been going twenty-five years next year and my happy customers run into the thousands.'

'Well done, Mr Letcher. We're investigating the murder of Chief Inspector Llewellyn-Dalrymple.'

His eyebrows raised. 'You're investigating it, are you? You don't look like detectives to me.'

'My name is Mrs Churchill, and this is my assistant, Miss Pemberley.'

'It's a pleasure to meet you. Now perhaps you can tell me what sort of motor car you're looking for. A tourer for leisure, perhaps?'

'We're not looking for a motor car at the moment, Mr Letcher. Did you attend Inspector Mappin's retirement party at the weekend?'

'Yes, I was there. Terribly sad about old Llewellyn-Dalrymple, isn't it? I wasn't expecting that.'

'Nobody was expecting it. It was very tragic. We're making some inquiries around the village to find out if anybody knew who might have wanted to murder him.'

'Have you got any names?'

'Not yet. Have you any ideas about it, Mr Letcher?'

He pushed out his lower lip and shook his head. 'None.'

'Can you think of any reason why someone would want to murder him?'

'No, I'm afraid not. I can't help you any more than that.'

'We understand there was a grievance between him and the Beanfork family after he ensured Fred Beanfork was convicted for robbing Mr Gilding's jeweller's shop.'

'Was there? I wouldn't know anything about that.' He scratched his chin.

'You don't remember the robbery three years ago?'

He shook his head. 'No, I don't remember it. I don't pay a lot of attention to what happens in the village. I just mind my own business here in my garage. So I'm sorry I haven't been able to help you any more than that.'

'Very well. Well, we appreciate your time speaking to us. Oh, there's just one other thing—we spoke to Mr Gilding and he says that his first thought when the robber stepped into the shop was that he was you, Mr Letcher.'

'Me?' He laughed. 'Why would I rob a jeweller's shop?'

'I really don't know you well enough to say, Mr Letcher.'

'Well, it's a very odd thing for Mr Gilding to claim, given that I don't know the man at all and have never met him. In fact, I didn't even know there was a jeweller's shop in the village. So that just goes to show how much I know about all this. Now then, if you two ladies aren't here to buy a motor car or avail yourself of the other garage services I offer, then I suggest you toddle off. I don't need you wasting my time any more today.'

As Churchill and Pemberley left the garage, Churchill glanced at the sombre undertaker's shop opposite.

'I wonder what it's like having an undertaker as a man friend?' she said. 'I can't imagine Mr Greystone being a barrel of laughs.'

'Mr Letcher isn't a barrel of laughs either,' said Pemberley. 'He got quite unpleasant with us, didn't he?'

'It's because we put him on the spot, Pembers. He didn't like it. Having spoken to him, I'm growing increasingly convinced that he's the one who robbed Mr Gilding's shop and Fred Beanfork is innocent. No wonder Fred and his mother hated Llewellyn-Dalrymple so much. And as for Letcher's claim he didn't even know there was a jeweller's shop in the village… well, that's just nonsense! We need to speak to Inspector Mappin about this and see what he makes of him. And did you notice Letcher's eyes, Pemberley?'

'No. I didn't want to look at them.'

'They're blue. Just as Mr Gilding described.'

Chapter Fifteen

AT THE POLICE STATION, INSPECTOR MAPPIN AND Inspector Kendall were arguing about desks. A second desk had appeared in the office since Churchill and Pemberley's last visit, and there was barely any room to walk around the furniture.

'There's no room for it, Kendall!' said Mappin.

'There is if you move yours over a foot.'

'My desk has been in that position for over fifteen years,' said Mappin. 'And I'm not about to move it now. Especially not for an interloper.'

'Interloper?' said Kendall. 'You're supposed to be retired. I'm the one who should be sitting at your desk. I'm your replacement, remember? If you retire, then we won't need two desks in here.'

'Golly,' said Churchill. 'What a palaver.'

'Yes, it is,' said Mappin, looking red-faced and flustered. 'This force has just been landed the most serious investigation in my entire career, and Kendall here is making a fuss about desks!'

'Have you got a moment to discuss Mr Letcher, Inspector?'

'What's he done now?'

'I don't know. But did you ever have any doubts about Fred Beanfork's conviction for burgling Mr Gilding's jewellery shop?'

Kendall stepped over to his desk to move it. Mappin quickly sat on it to stop him. 'No, Mrs Churchill. No doubts whatsoever. Chief Inspector Llewellyn-Dalrymple was quite convinced young Fred was the man responsible, and so he was punished accordingly.'

'But Mr Gilding confided to us he thought, first of all, that the man who robbed his shop that day was actually Mr Letcher.'

'Yes, I recall Mr Gilding saying such a thing at the time.'

Churchill's heart gave a flip. 'You do? So why was Fred Beanfork arrested?'

'Because we thought his alibi was lying.'

'Why?'

'Because he seemed the sort. To be honest with you, Mrs Churchill, it's an investigation which Chief Inspector Llewellyn-Dalrymple took over. I began making inquiries, but Llewellyn-Dalrymple told me he would manage it all.'

'Surely you were capable of investigating?' said Churchill. 'Why did he get involved?'

'Yes, it seemed odd at the time. But he told me he had information that Fred Beanfork was the culprit, so I deferred to him. He was my superior, and that was the way things worked. It's the chain of command, you see.'

'Did the chief inspector suspect Mr Letcher at all?'

'No. He was always keen to defend the man.'

'Why? From what I've heard, Letcher is a seasoned criminal.'

'Oh yes, he's been up to all sorts of trouble over the years—poaching, trespassing, stealing livestock, stealing motor cars, illegal gambling, impersonating an official, selling watered-down alcohol, cashing bad cheques… The list goes on and on.'

'Good grief. Has he ever been punished for anything?'

Mappin gave this some thought. 'I'm not sure he has. I collared him for a few things, but each time Chief Inspector Llewellyn-Dalrymple told me to drop the matter.'

Churchill exchanged an incredulous look with Pemberley. Then she turned back to the inspector. 'Why did he tell you to do that?'

'Various reasons. On one occasion, I was told my inquiries were endangering a larger investigation which the chief inspector was in charge of. Another time I was told there wasn't enough evidence. And he once told me a case would require too much paperwork to be worth it's while and that I should drop it. So I did.'

'Did you not think that was all a bit fishy?'

'Not really. Chief Inspector Llewellyn-Dalrymple was my superior, and he knew best.'

'Do you think the chief inspector was protecting Letcher?'

'I suppose you could view it like that, but I don't think he was. That would have been unprofessional.'

'It sounds to me he purposefully stopped you from investigating Mr Letcher's illicit activities,' said Churchill. 'Were the two men friends?'

'Friends? No. Of course not.'

'I see. Well, there was something funny going on there, that's for sure.'

Mappin got to his feet. 'Kendall! What are you doing?'

'Emptying your filing cabinet, Mappin. I need to move it.'

'No, you don't!'

Churchill turned to Pemberley, shaking her head. 'Hapless,' she whispered. 'Come along. Let's go.'

Back at the office, Churchill rested her weary feet on her desk and had a doze. A short while later, the shrill ring of the telephone awoke her.

'Great Scott!' Her heart thudded in her chest and her face flushed hot. 'There's nothing quite as awful as being woken by a ringing telephone. Why's it so loud?'

She lifted the receiver to stop it ringing and took a moment to catch her breath.

'Hello?' whined a small voice from the receiver.

Churchill put it to her ear. 'Hello?' she said. 'Who's this?'

'Mrs Thonnings.'

'Why are you telephoning me?'

'It's quicker than walking there. I was just wondering how you're getting on with finding out how Mrs Honeypear stole my simnel cake recipe.'

Churchill sighed and pinched the bridge of her nose.

'Mrs Churchill?'

'Yes, I can hear you, Mrs Thonnings. Don't worry, I'm working hard on it.'

'Oh good. Shall I expect an update from you soon then?'

'Yes, very soon. Goodbye Mrs Thonnings.' She put down the receiver and turned to Pemberley. 'I couldn't care less about this simnel cake recipe, but I suppose Mrs Thonnings has tasked us with looking into it, so there we go. Shall we visit your friend Miss Applethorn?'

'Oh yes! Let's!' Pemberley clapped her palms together with glee.

'Good. She's a member of the Ladies Sewing Circle and might have seen who copied down that recipe.'

Chapter Sixteen

CHURCHILL AND PEMBERLEY FOUND MISS APPLETHORN behind her desk in the library.

'Oh, this is a pleasant surprise!' she said. 'Look, Whisker, your friend Oswald is here!'

Whisker stepped out from behind the desk, his tail wagging furiously. He and Oswald sniffed noses, then scampered off to the non-fiction section together.

'I didn't realise dogs are allowed in libraries,' said Churchill.

'The head librarian told me it was permitted as long as Whisker behaves himself.'

'I see.' Churchill gave a sniff and pulled up a nearby chair. 'We're investigating the theft of a cake recipe,' she said.

The librarian's jaw dropped in horror. 'It wasn't me!'

'We're not accusing you of anything, Miss Applethorn. But you may be a useful witness.'

'I didn't see anyone steal a recipe,' she said, her eyes wide with worry.

'Let me explain,' said Pemberley, also pulling up a

chair. Miss Applethorn's shoulders relaxed a little as Pemberley told her about the stolen recipe. 'We believe you visited Mrs Thonnings's home recently because you're a member of the Ladies Sewing Circle.'

'That's right.' She broke out into a smile. 'I'm sewing a little hat for Whisker.'

'A little hat? Oh, how lovely. I would like to make one for Oswald!'

'Then you must join us, Miss Pemberley. And the dogs can have matching hats!'

'Wouldn't they look lovely together?'

'Oh, they would!'

Churchill felt her jaw clench. 'Let's get back to the matter at hand,' she said. 'When you were at the most recent gathering of the Ladies Sewing Circle, did you notice anybody poking around in the dresser?'

'No.'

'Mrs Thonnings seems to think the opportunity to copy down the recipe may have arisen while everyone was having tea and biscuits in the front room. Do you recall anyone leaving the room while you were there?'

'I think a few people left the room to use the lavatory.'

'Can you recall who?'

'No.'

'Did you leave the front room at all during tea and biscuits?'

'No.'

'Did you notice anyone with a pen or pencil and a notebook?' asked Pemberley.

'That's an excellent question, Miss Pemberley,' said Churchill. 'The person in question must have taken a notebook with them to copy down the recipe.'

'I don't remember seeing anybody with a notebook,' said Miss Applethorn.

'How well do you know Mrs Honeypear?' asked Churchill.

'I don't know her at all. But I've visited her tea rooms a few times and had some very nice tea and cake there.'

'Do you know of anyone in the Ladies Sewing Circle who could be a good friend of Mrs Honeypear?'

Miss Applethorn shook her head. 'No.'

Churchill gave an inward sigh. Miss Applethorn knew nothing whatsoever. 'Well, thank you for your time. If you recall anything useful from the most recent gathering of the Ladies Sewing Circle, then you'll let Miss Pemberley or myself know, won't you?'

'Oh, absolutely. When I get home, I shall have a long, hard think about it all and try to remember if I saw anything suspicious that day.'

'Thank you, Miss Applethorn.'

'And thank you to you too, Mrs Churchill, for allowing me to be second on your waiting list.'

Churchill sighed and gave Pemberley a sidelong glance.

'I don't know if Miss Pemberley mentioned it to you, but I would simply love to become a detective,' continued Miss Applethorn. 'She said there were no vacancies with your detective agency at the moment, but you have a waiting list. She told me Mrs Thonnings is first on the waiting list and I'm second.'

Churchill clenched her jaw. Pemberley had clearly misunderstood their conversation about the waiting list. She wished now she'd never mentioned it to her. 'There's not really a waiting list,' she said. 'We were having a hypothetical discussion.'

'Oh, I see.' Miss Applethorn's face fell. 'That's a shame, because I've been getting my hopes up. Anyway, never mind. If you do need a hand with any investigating, then you will let me know, won't you?'

'I will, Miss Applethorn.'

'Anyway, I'm sure you'll solve the case of the stolen recipe. Poor Mrs Thonnings. I don't understand how people can be so heartless.' She turned to Pemberley. 'Talking of heartless, I've got to that chapter in David Copperfield now, Miss Pemberley.'

'Oh really? What did you think?'

'Heartless.'

'I knew it.'

Churchill pursed her lips and drummed her fingers on her handbag as the two ladies talked earnestly about the book.

After a few minutes, she got to her feet, rounded up the dogs, and returned to the desk. 'Right then, we need to get on, Miss Pemberley.'

'Get on with what?'

'Work.'

'Oh yes.' Pemberley got to her feet. 'Are you still alright for backgammon tonight, Miss Applethorn?'

'Oh yes. Absolutely.'

Churchill's lips were pursed so hard they ached. She didn't know Pemberley and Miss Applethorn had made plans to play backgammon and she felt a little left out. 'Come along,' she said stiffly. 'It's almost the end of the day and there's still so much we haven't done.'

Shopkeepers were bringing in their displays and folding up their awnings as Churchill and Pemberley walked back to their office.

'How nice of Miss Applethorn to be so helpful,' said Pemberley.

'Helpful, Pemberley? She knew nothing!'

'But she gave up her time to speak to us.'

'Yes, but she was hardly run off her feet in the library, was she? And she didn't give us anything useful whatsoever. She's either completely unobservant or she's covering for someone.'

'Miss Applethorn would never cover for anyone! She's an extremely honest lady!'

'Well, that's reassuring to know then. But the fact is, she didn't see anyone acting suspiciously there that day.'

'Mrs Thonnings could be mistaken. We could be going to all this effort to find someone who supposedly copied down the recipe when, in fact, nobody copied it down at all.'

'Actually, you're right,' said Churchill. 'Mrs Thonnings swears it's her family recipe, but one simnel cake tastes much like another as far as I'm concerned. They're all equally delicious. However, Mrs Thonnings maintains the recipe was shuffled about in her sewing basket. And let's not forget she's paying us for our time.'

'Is she?'

'Yes. So, like it or not, Pembers, we need to get to the bottom of this.'

Chapter Seventeen

Churchill and Pemberley called on Mrs Thonnings in her haberdashery shop the following morning. They found her rearranging embroidery threads in a colourful display.

'Oh hello, lady detectives!' She beamed. 'So have you found who stole the recipe?'

'We spoke to Miss Applethorn about it,' said Churchill.

The haberdasher gasped. 'She stole it! I don't believe it. Miss Applethorn?'

'No. She doesn't know who stole it.'

'Oh.'

'She couldn't tell us anything, I'm afraid. But I thought I'd report back to you to let you know that.'

'I see.' Mrs Thonnings looked glum.

'But we shall keep on with our enquiries, don't you worry.'

The bell above the door rang, and a customer stepped into the shop. She had an upturned nose and wore a black hat.

'Mrs Llewellyn-Dalrymple!' said Mrs Thonnings. 'How are you?'

The widow gave a sniff. 'I've been better.'

'Yes, I can imagine. But it's nice to see you out and about. It's much better than sitting at home. Perhaps you're looking to start a new sewing project to cheer yourself up?'

'Yes. It will keep me busy. But it won't cheer me up.'

'That's not surprising at all,' said Churchill. 'At times like this, it's difficult to feel cheered up by anything. It takes time.'

'It does indeed.' She glanced around the shop as if deciding which display to look at first.

'Miss Pemberley and I have decided to investigate your husband's death because the local constabulary seems rather disorganised,' added Churchill.

Mrs Llewellyn-Dalrymple frowned. 'Really? I'm sure there's no need. Inspector Kendall and Inspector Mappin will sort it out between themselves, and they're reporting to Superintendent Trowelbank for the time being. The police force is organised enough to deal with the loss of a man.'

'Well, that's good to hear,' said Churchill, not wanting to disagree with her. 'This may sound like an odd question, but was your late husband friends with Mr Letcher?'

Mrs Llewellyn-Dalrymple wrinkled her nose. 'Mr Letcher? The man who runs that garage on the South Bungerly Road? No, the two were never friends.'

'I didn't think so. But it's been suggested to me that your husband had a lenient attitude towards Mr Letcher's misdemeanours.'

The widow puffed out her chest. 'How dare you! My husband was never lenient towards anyone!'

'I see. I'm sorry if my words have offended you, Mrs Llewellyn-Dalrymple. It was just a rumour, but clearly it isn't true.'

'No, it's not true at all. My husband was a respectable and responsible chief inspector. He was highly thought of by absolutely everyone who knew him. If he thought Mr Letcher had done something wrong, then I'm sure he would have charged him with it and ensured he was locked up for a very long time.'

'I'm sure he would have done. I'm sorry to bring it up, really. The next time I hear someone suggest such a thing, I shall correct them.'

'Please do, Mrs Churchill. It's extremely distressing for me.' She pulled out a handkerchief and dabbed at her eyes. 'Has your new delivery of ribbon arrived yet, Mrs Thonnings?'

'Yes, it has, Mrs Llewellyn-Dalrymple,' said the haberdasher, taking her by the arm. 'I've got some lovely new supplies. Come and have a look at them.'

Churchill and Pemberley skulked around by the sewing machine display while Mrs Thonnings and Mrs Llewellyn-Dalrymple discussed ribbon. Once the widow had made her purchases and left, Mrs Thonnings approached them. 'Goodness me, Mrs Churchill, what a question you asked her! You accused her recently deceased husband of being friendly with a criminal!'

'I didn't enjoy upsetting her,' said Churchill. 'But I was only repeating what Inspector Mappin suggested. He gave us a great long list of crimes which Mr Letcher had committed, and the late chief inspector had countless excuses why the police shouldn't prosecute him.'

'Crikey, did he really? Well, we all know Letcher is no good. And now you come to mention it, it's interesting he's never been punished for anything. And that could be down to Chief Inspector Llewellyn-Dalrymple, you think?'

'Possibly. Although his wife denies it, obviously.'

'Well, she would,' said Mrs Thonnings. 'She doesn't

want to admit her late husband wasn't doing his job properly.'

Mrs Thonnings straightened a sewing machine on the shelf and lowered her voice. 'If you ask me, I think Mrs Llewellyn-Dalrymple is acting more upset than she actually is.'

'Really?' said Churchill.

'Yes. Their marriage wasn't happy for a long time,' said Mrs Thonnings. 'I don't know why. But Mrs Llewellyn-Dalrymple rarely looked cheerful when they were together.'

'Perhaps she's the morose type,' said Pemberley.

'Possibly,' said Mrs Thonnings. 'I may be speaking out of turn here, but Mrs Llewellyn-Dalrymple is doing a good job of parading around in her widow's weeds and looking jollier than she has in a long time.'

Churchill frowned. 'Really?'

Mrs Thonnings nodded. 'I think she's quite relieved her husband is dead.'

Chapter Eighteen

Churchill and Pemberley surveyed their incident board when they returned to their office.

'Now then, Pembers,' said Churchill. 'Shall we consider Mrs Llewellyn-Dalrymple as a suspect? That admission from Mrs Thonnings just then was remarkable. Mrs Llewellyn-Dalrymple is relieved her husband is dead! Do you think that could be true?'

'I can imagine it being true,' said Pemberley. 'Mrs Thonnings knows her better than I do, so I'm happy to take her word for it.'

'Me too. And this could mean that Mrs Llewellyn-Dalrymple murdered her husband in the refreshments tent. It wouldn't have been difficult to do, would it? While they were watching the Morris dancers, she could have suggested in his ear that they sidle off to get some cake and then… bam! He wouldn't have known another thing.'

'She would have had to really dislike him to do that,' said Pemberley. 'We need evidence that was the case.'

'We do. And that could involve speaking to a lot of people. But let's find a picture of her for now and pin her to our board. And there's Mr Letcher to consider too. There was clearly some funny business between him and the chief inspector.'

'I think Letcher had something on him,' said Pemberley.

'What do you mean by that?'

'Perhaps Llewellyn-Dalrymple owed him a large favour. Or maybe Letcher knew some secret information about the chief inspector.'

'Yes!' said Churchill. 'That could be it! It explains why Letcher could commit as many crimes as he liked. He knew he wouldn't be punished.'

Pemberley nodded. 'Because if he was punished, then he could reveal the secret information about Llewellyn-Dalrymple.'

'Blackmail, Pembers!'

'Corruption.'

'But if Letcher was blackmailing Llewellyn-Dalrymple,' said Churchill. 'Why could he have murdered him?'

'Maybe something changed,' said Pemberley. 'Maybe Llewellyn-Dalrymple got fed up with having to let Letcher get away scot-free and decided he was going to prosecute him for something.'

'An excellent suggestion. The arrangement could have harmoniously existed between them for a while, but then Llewellyn-Dalrymple decided he was finally going to do something about Letcher's crimes. Letcher didn't take too kindly to the idea and hit Llewellyn-Dalrymple over the head with a large teapot. That makes sense. And having met Mr Letcher, I can see how he might turn unpleasant quite quickly.'

'Oh yes, he would. In fact, the more I think about it, Mrs Churchill, the more convinced I am that he's the murderer.'

'So what should our next steps be, Pembers? I can't say I want to ask Mr Letcher directly about any of this, he won't take kindly to it.'

'No, he won't.'

'Ideally, I'd like to get inside that garage of his and have a rummage around for evidence that he and Llewellyn-Dalrymple had an arrangement of some sort.'

'You want to go in there?' Pemberley shuddered. 'You wouldn't catch me in there!'

'These things have to be done if we're going to find evidence. Is there an opportunity to get into that garage while Letcher is absent?'

'I've no idea!'

'Me neither. But I'll tell you how we find out, Pemberley. We put Letcher's Garage under surveillance.'

'Oh, how exciting. I love surveillance!'

'Good. Because I think we're going to be doing quite a lot in the coming days.'

'How are we going to do it?'

'It's quite simple. Letcher's premises are overlooked by Mr Greystone's funeral parlour on the opposite side of the road. All we need to do is ask Mrs Thonnings to ask him if we can position ourselves at his upstairs window. With a bit of luck, he'll agree to it.'

'I'm sure he will,' said Pemberley. 'He's a pleasant gentleman. He's buried quite a few of my friends, actually.'

'Oh.' Churchill felt her shoulders sink. She didn't like being reminded of her own mortality. 'Anyway. Let's put this plan into action, Pembers, and see what we can find out about dodgy Mr Letcher and his connection to a senior police officer.'

Chapter Nineteen

AFTER A TELEPHONE CALL TO MRS THONNINGS, THE surveillance plan at the undertakers was arranged.

The following day, Churchill and Pemberley called on Mr Greystone with a picnic basket of supplies and Oswald in tow.

A heaviness weighed on Churchill as they stepped into the funeral parlour. It was eerily quiet with comfortable seating, the scent of lilies and muted colours. 'I hope it's a long time before I need the services of a place like this,' she whispered to Pemberley.

'Death comes to all of us, Mrs Churchill.'

Churchill felt the weight on her shoulders grow heavier.

A lean, sombre man emerged silently from a doorway. 'Good morning ladies, how may I help?' He was soft-spoken and reverential.

Churchill introduced themselves, and his face brightened. 'Oh, of course!' His voice rose a few decibels, and he grinned. 'Mrs Thonnings spoke to me about you yesterday. And that

The Teapot Killer

explains why you've brought a picnic hamper with you. Supplies!' He gave a loud laugh which seemed at odds with their surroundings. 'I assumed you were new customers given your appearance... oops, sorry. That was tactless of me.'

'You mean we're old, Mr Greystone,' said Churchill. 'And therefore more likely to know someone who's died.' She was feeling worse by the minute. She could only hope the cherry cake she'd packed in their picnic hamper would cheer her up.

'What do you know about Mr Letcher over the road?' Pemberley asked him.

'Not a lot. He's not my type, but we've both been running our respective businesses here for almost twenty-five years. You hear occasional stories about things he's been mixed up in. But I've never witnessed him do anything criminal myself, so I choose not to pass judgment.'

'Well, it pays to get on with one's neighbours, doesn't it?' said Churchill. 'Did you ever see Chief Inspector Llewellyn-Dalrymple visit Mr Letcher?'

'The police inspector who died at Inspector Mappin's retirement party? Yes, I saw him at Letcher's Garage a few times. We're handling his funeral arrangements, actually. His widow was here yesterday choosing the coffin. She's gone for walnut with the quilted satin lining, brass fittings and the engraved nameplate.'

Churchill shifted uncomfortably. 'Has she? I see.'

'Our quilted linings have become more popular in recent years. They provide extra comfort.'

'Comfort?'

'The families of the deceased are reassured by the comfort. Even if it's of little benefit to the deceased themselves.'

'I'm pleased to hear it. So how often did you see Chief Inspector Llewellyn-Dalrymple visiting Mr Letcher?'

'Only two or three times. He wasn't a regular visitor. But I recall the visits because I remember thinking Letcher must be in extra big trouble if he had top brass visiting him.'

'Interesting. But he never seems to get into trouble, does he? It certainly is a puzzle. Thank you for allowing us to use your upstairs room for surveillance.'

'It's no trouble at all,' said Mr Greystone. 'Friends of Mrs Thonnings are friends of mine.'

'We're extremely grateful,' said Churchill. 'Before we get settled in, I'm wondering if you know anything about Mrs Thonnings's simnel cake recipe?'

He sighed. 'Ah yes, she thinks the lady in the tea rooms stole it from her, doesn't she?' He shook his head. 'I've told her it can't be the same recipe, it must be a similar one.'

Churchill nodded. 'I've told her the same. But she's tasked us with investigating, so that's what we shall do. Did you happen to see the simnel cake recipe anywhere when you last visited her?'

'No. Not that I know of. What does it look like?'

'It's a piece of paper with the recipe written down on it. It's got a few grease marks and spatters on it.'

'No, I didn't see it. I'm afraid I don't take much interest in cake recipes. Shall I show you the room upstairs? Allow me to carry your picnic basket for you.'

The two ladies and their dog followed the undertaker up the stairs and to the room at the front of the building which overlooked the road and Letcher's Garage opposite.

'We use this as a storage room, as you can see,' said Mr Greystone. 'So it's a bit cluttered, but I've put two chairs by the window.'

Cardboard boxes were stacked on top of each other

and shelves lined the walls. A shiny wooden coffin lid rested against a wall, and model headstones were stacked in a corner.

'I'm afraid there might be a bit of noise today,' said Mr Greystone. 'My son's got a coffin to make. He's in the workshop out the back, so he won't trouble you at all. Obviously, he stops work when we have bereaved visitors, but he has to get on with the business at hand.'

Churchill thanked him and made herself comfortable on one of the chairs. 'Ah yes, this is an excellent view,' she said to Pemberley. 'We can see everything from this spot.'

Pemberley sat down next to her with Oswald on her lap. Rolls of black, white and red satin fabric were propped against the shelves behind her.

'Do you think that's material for lining coffins with?' Churchill asked with a shiver.

'Yes it must be,' said Pemberley. 'I can't see the quilted option there though, perhaps it's in the workshop with Mr Greystone's son. Oh look! Someone's arrived at Letcher's Garage for petrol.' She took her field glasses out of her bag and peered out of the window.

Churchill tore her eyes away from the coffin linings and did the same. A bottle green Hillman Minx car was parked by one of the petrol pumps.

'Here comes Mr Letcher now,' said Pemberley.

They watched as he stepped out of his kiosk, spoke with the driver, then proceeded to fill the car with petrol.

'Nothing suspicious so far,' said Pemberley.

'No. But we've only been sitting here for five minutes. We must be patient.'

After the Hillman had left the garage, everything was quiet for a while. Churchill smoothed her skirt, and her mind turned to the food and drink in the picnic hamper. 'We mustn't start on our refreshments too early, Pembers, otherwise they won't last. I think we should wait at least an hour before we get started on them.'

'Good idea, Mrs Churchill.'

Churchill examined the pile of boxes next to her chair and read the writing on them. '"Post mortem and cavity chemical",' she said. 'Oh golly, Pembers. This is embalming fluid!'

'We're in the storage room of a funeral parlour, Mrs Churchill. We have to expect these things.'

'I suppose so. It's a shame there isn't a nice bakery opposite Letcher's Garage, isn't it?' Her mouth usually watered when she thought of bakeries, but the embalming fluid had suppressed her appetite.

After an hour, Churchill stretched her legs by pacing the room. She tried to ignore the items around her, but it was difficult. A box of shrouds sat open—a shroud had been taken out and was resting on top. Wreaths of artificial flowers rested on the shelves next to a box of black ostrich feathers.

'Do you think it's time for sandwiches and tea, Mrs Churchill?' asked Pemberley.

'Yes, I suppose it is.'

'You don't sound as keen as usual.'

'No, I don't have much of an appetite at the moment. Perhaps the sight of a cheese sandwich will change that.'

But the cheese sandwich took a while to eat. No matter how enthusiastic Churchill tried to be about it, her stomach remained disinterested. 'I'll have the rest later,' she said, wrapping it in its paper bag.

Pemberley gave her a concerned look. 'Are you feeling alright, Mrs Churchill?'

'Yes. I'm fine.'

'Are you sure?'

'Yes. There's just something about this place which…

oh, never mind, Pembers. I just don't like the thought of dying, that's all. I pray I'm spared a few more years yet.'

'I'm sure you will be.' Pemberley leafed through a book in her lap while Oswald dozed beneath her chair.

'What book is that, Pembers?'

'It's a book of epitaphs which you can have put on your gravestone. I like this one, "The song has ended, but the melody lingers on."'

'Oh goodness, that sounds rather sad.'

'Or there's "A flower picked before its time." I'd like that on my gravestone.'

'Picked before your time, Pembers? You've already been around for a lot of time.'

'There's no need to be rude, Mrs Churchill.'

'I'm not being rude. I'm just stating the obvious. By the time you finally turn up your toes, Pembers, no one will say you were picked before your time.'

'No matter how much time I get, I'll always want more,' said Pemberley.

'Alright then. Fair enough. Oh look, is Mr Letcher going somewhere?'

The garage owner was wheeling a motorcycle out of his shed. The two ladies watched as he put on a pair of goggles and climbed astride it. Then he started the engine and took off down the road.

'Where's he gone?' said Churchill. 'And who's going to look after the garage now?'

Her question was answered when a red Riley Kestrel pulled up at the garage and a woman in overalls and a headscarf emerged from the kiosk.

'Who's she?' asked Churchill, peering at the lady through her field glasses. 'A wife or a co-worker?'

'I don't know,' said Pemberley. 'I've never seen her before in my life.'

Chapter Twenty

CHURCHILL AND PEMBERLEY CARRIED OUT THEIR surveillance of Letcher's Garage for three days. During that time, they realised Mr Letcher left the garage every afternoon at two o'clock and returned at five o'clock. During his absence, the lady in the overalls and headscarf looked after the garage.

'I wonder where Mr Letcher goes every afternoon,' said Churchill. 'Perhaps that's the time when he gets up to all his criminal activities and then he returns to his garage again. I wonder what he gets up to in the evenings?'

'He probably sits at home with his feet up listening to the wireless.'

'That's what normal people do, Pembers. But not crooks like Mr Letcher. Nighttime is usually the time when they really get up to mischief. I think we need to stay here a little later today and see what Letcher does tonight.'

Pemberley's face fell. 'Really?'

'Yes, Pembers. It's just one evening. Let's go back to our respective homes for our evening meals, then meet here again at eight.'

The Teapot Killer

Pemberley sighed. 'Alright then. And once we've done that, can we end our surveillance?'

'If we feel we have enough information by the end of the evening, then yes.'

Churchill and Pemberley resumed their surveillance positions that evening. Once the sun had set, darkness spread from the corners of the storeroom. The back of Churchill's neck felt chilly, and she couldn't stop thinking about the box of shrouds and the coffin linings which shared the room with them.

'There's no one at the garage,' said Pemberley. 'I knew it. Letcher's at home listening to his wireless.'

The following two hours dragged interminably. The room turned dark. Churchill sipped tea from the flask, nibbled biscuits and encouraged Pemberley to keep going as all hope seemed lost.

Eventually, they heard the distant sound of the motorcycle on the road.

'He's back!' hissed Churchill with excitement. She picked up her field glasses and watched as the motorcycle stopped at the garage. There was little light to see by, but there was soon more when Letcher turned on the lights in the kiosk.

'So now what?' said Pemberley.

'Let's see if anyone else turns up,' said Churchill.

A short while later, a dark motor car arrived at the garage.

'It's a dark blue Austin Ten,' said Pemberley as she peered through her field glasses. 'And I can see a lady getting out.'

'A lady visitor at this hour?' Churchill peered through her field glasses, but it was too dark to see much. 'Oh, darn it, Pemberley, this is annoying. It's not light enough to see who that lady is. Can you see the number plate?'

'No, I can't.'

'Right then, I'm going to go outside and have a closer look. You and Oswald can keep watch up here, Pemberley.'

'But what if they see you?'

'They won't. I'm very good at lurking in the shadows.'

Churchill made her way downstairs and stepped out of the funeral parlour and into the quiet road. Light from the garage kiosk lit her way as she approached the car. Pemberley had been right about the make and model of it. She took a pen and notebook out of her handbag and wrote down the number plate.

'Mrs Churchill? This is a surprise.'

Her heart leapt into her mouth.

Turning, she saw Mrs Llewellyn-Dalrymple in the doorway of the kiosk.

Flustered, Churchill hurriedly put her notebook and pen back in her handbag. 'So it is indeed! Hello, Mrs Llewellyn-Dalrymple. I didn't see you there. What are you doing at Mr Letcher's garage at this time of night?'

'I could ask the same of you.'

'Yes, you could. I was just taking an evening stroll along the road. It's a pleasant evening, isn't it?'

'Yes. I saw you looking at my car.'

'I was trying to work out if I recognised it or not.'

'Oh, I see. Yes, there's a problem with its gears, so I've asked Mr Letcher to have a look at it for me.'

'At ten o'clock in the evening?'

'Yes. It's been such a busy day—I've had so much to sort out. He said he would be here all evening, so I thought I'd drop in.'

Mr Letcher joined her in the doorway.

'Taking an evening stroll,' replied Churchill through gritted teeth. She felt angry her surveillance had gone wrong.

'Excellent. Well, don't let us keep you, then.'

'No, absolutely not.' She glanced up and down the road, deciding which way she was supposed to be walking. 'Well, I'll just continue along here, then.'

'Very good. Enjoy your walk.'

Unfortunately for Churchill, the road was long and straight, and Mrs Llewellyn-Dalrymple and Mr Letcher had full view of her for quite a while. She dared not glance back to check if they were still watching in case it made her look suspicious.

Once she'd covered two hundred yards, she paused by a doorway and looked back. There was no sign of them now. But she didn't want to risk walking back to the funeral parlour for a while in case they spotted her again. Churchill stood in the doorway and waited.

Fifteen minutes passed before Mrs Llewellyn-Dalrymple's motor car pulled away from the garage. Churchill pressed herself up against the door as the car passed her. Then she hurried back to Pemberley.

'What on earth happened, Mrs Churchill? I saw you speaking to Mrs Llewellyn-Dalrymple and Mr Letcher, then you walked off.'

'I had to pretend I was taking an evening stroll, Pemberley. Did you see what they got up to?'

'Mr Letcher opened the bonnet of the car and fiddled about for a bit. Then Mrs Llewellyn-Dalrymple drove off.'

'Interesting,' said Churchill. 'But why would he do such a thing at ten o'clock in the evening?'

Chapter Twenty-One

'I've got a plan,' said Churchill the following morning as she and Pemberley had a cup of tea and a slice of lemon cake. 'We need to get inside Letcher's Garage.'

'Why?'

'Because I want to find some evidence that he's up to no good. I'm tired of him doing whatever he wants with no repercussions. And there's something very odd about Mrs Llewellyn-Dalrymple's late-night visit. We know she's been visiting Greystone's funeral parlour to arrange her husband's funeral, so why didn't she call at the garage at the same time? Why wait until late in the evening?'

'I don't see how we're going to find the answers inside Letcher's garage.'

'We might or we might not. But we at least need to try while Letcher is out for the afternoon. The lady who works there doesn't know who we are, so we can disguise ourselves as motoring ladies.'

'Motoring ladies?'

'Yes. Those motoring enthusiasts who like driving

across the country in their goggles and gloves, Pemberley. That's what we need to pretend to be.'

'But we don't have a motor car.'

'Do you know anyone who has a car we can borrow?'

'Well, there's my cousin Bertie who lives in South Bungerly. He has an Austin Seven Chummy Tourer which he hardly ever uses.'

'Perfect. Let's see if we can borrow it.'

'He'll expect payment.'

'Payment? Even though he's your cousin?'

'I'm afraid so. My family is a bit like that. It's the reason I have as little to do with them as possible.'

A few hours later, the two ladies left South Bungerly village in Pemberley's cousin's sky-blue motor car. The sun was shining and Pemberley had folded the roof down. Both ladies wore motoring caps, goggles and gloves.

Churchill held onto her cap and gripped her seat as they flew along the country lanes. Oswald sat on her lap, his little ears swept back by the wind.

'Pemberley, I wish you'd slow down a little!' shouted Churchill over the noise of the engine.

'I'm not going fast, Mrs Churchill!'

Churchill screwed her eyes shut as they headed towards a sharp end. Then cautiously opened them again once the road straightened. 'You can't possibly see what's around the corner!'

'You develop an instinct when you drive along country roads a lot.'

'Instinct? You're trusting your instinct rather than using your actual sight?'

Pemberley braked so suddenly that Churchill had to grab Oswald as she was flung forward in her seat. As they rounded the bend, they saw a horse and cart labouring up the hill towards them.

'There you go,' said Pemberley. 'That's an example of my instinct. I knew that horse and cart were there.'

Churchill felt too shaken to respond. She recovered herself as Pemberley edged the car up against the hedgerow and twigs scraped the paintwork. The driver of the cart gave a grateful wave and lumbered past.

Pemberley pressed her foot on the accelerator and they were off again.

'I shall just close my eyes for the rest of the journey,' said Churchill. 'I can't bear it.'

Ten minutes later, Mr Letcher's garage appeared up ahead.

'Here we are,' said Pemberley, braking sharply. 'What shall I say to the lady who works here?'

'I'm sure you'll think of something, Pemberley. Just detain her while I look inside the garage.'

'At times like this, my mind goes blank and my mouth freezes,' said Pemberley. 'Then I really don't know what to say.'

'You're a detective, Pembers. You can't possibly freeze and say nothing. Just act like a motoring lady.'

The lady in the overalls and headscarf stepped out of the kiosk. She had a glum, lined face with narrow eyes.

Churchill pushed her goggles up onto her motoring cap. 'Good afternoon! It's a lovely day for a drive, isn't it?'

'Suppose it is,' said the lady. 'How much do you want putting in?'

'Oh, I'm not sure. Please consult with my friend, the driver, here. In the meantime, I was wondering if you have a... ahem,' Churchill cleared her throat, 'little girls' room I may use? We've just been on a long drive, you see, and there haven't been many facilities along the way.'

The Teapot Killer

The lady jabbed her thumb at the large shed behind her. 'In there. It's the door at the back.'

'Thank you so much.'

Churchill moved Oswald onto Pemberley's lap and prayed her assistant would think of something to say to the lady to detain her. Churchill estimated she needed several minutes to look around inside the garage.

She stepped in through the doorway and was greeted with the smell of oil. Wooden beams supported the high ceiling and there were spills of dried oil on the concrete floor. A long wooden workbench was covered in tools, engine parts, and oil-stained rags. More tools were mounted on the wall. Rusty shelves housed battered cans of oil and paint and boxes of nuts, bolts, and screws. A tower of tyres was stacked against the wall and next to it was a crooked door with the letters "W.C." painted on.

Churchill headed for a small, untidy desk with a telephone and a calendar on the wall. Thankfully, she could hear Pemberley and the lady talking outside, so she still had some time.

Pulling out the drawers of the desk, she leafed through receipts and invoices, looking for something more interesting. She worked quickly, aware of the passing time. If she was too long, then the garage lady would grow suspicious.

Her heart thudded in her ears as she pulled out more drawers and looked through more papers. She reasoned she had little time left.

Then she came across some photographs. Most were photographs of cars, but some had people in. Churchill peered at them and gasped as she recognised the people in them.

The sound of an engine outside startled her. She pushed the drawers back and made her way over to the door marked "W.C.". She pulled open the door and was so appalled by the lack of cleanliness that she immediately closed it again.

She turned and was startled by a figure in front of her.

Mr Letcher.

Her mouth opened and closed. It was only three o'clock and she couldn't understand why he'd returned to the garage so early.

'Mrs Churchill? What are you doing in here?'

'I came in to use your facility.' She pointed at the door.

'That's very brave of you. It's blocked.'

'I came in here to use it, then changed my mind when I opened the door. I was just on my way out again.'

'That's your motor car by the petrol pumps, then.'

'My friend's car.' She stepped to the side to pass him. 'Well, it's been wonderful talking to you again, Mr Letcher, but I must be on my way.'

'You're becoming a regular visitor here, Mrs Churchill,' he said. 'Having never set eyes on you before this week, this is the third time I've seen you at my garage.'

'Has it really been three times? I'm impressed you've kept count, Mr Letcher.'

He stared at her as she left and she gave a little whistle, pretending she wasn't intimidated.

Outside, Pemberley was engaged in deep conversation with the garage lady.

'My sister had one who always barked at men with glasses,' said the lady. She was leaning against the car bonnet, her arms folded. 'If he met a lady with glasses, he didn't bark. But if he met a man with glasses, then that was it. He'd bark for hours.'

'Hours?' said Pemberley. 'Dear me.'

Churchill got back into the passenger seat. 'Let's go.' She didn't want to stay at Mr Letcher's garage any longer than she had to.

'Mrs Woodbine's sister had a Spanish water dog,' Pemberley explained.

'Good. Shall we go now?'

'She's got a cocker spaniel now and one that's half wire-haired fox terrier and half… oh, I can't remember now.'

'Never mind,' said Churchill, clenching her teeth with impatience. 'Just drive, Pembers,' she hissed.

Mr Letcher watched her from the doorway, his hands on his hips. She could feel his eyes boring into the side of her face.

'I can't drive off,' said Pemberley. 'Mrs Woodbine is leaning against the car and she's trying to remember the other half of her sister's dog.'

Churchill's jaw ached with frustration.

'I want to say Airedale terrier, but I don't think that's right,' said Mrs Woodbine.

'If you don't mind, we need to get going!' Churchill called out to Mrs Woodbine.

'Oh, right.' She stood upright. 'I think it might just be Scottish terrier. Yes, I think that's it. Half wire-haired fox terrier and half Scottish terrier.'

'So it's a terrier then,' said Churchill. 'How lovely. Bye, Mrs Woodbine!' She lowered her voice to a growl. 'Pembers, get us out of here.'

'Lovely meeting you!' Pemberley called out to Mrs Woodbine. Then she put her foot on the accelerator and slowly pulled away.

'Did you find anything inside the garage?' she asked Churchill.

'Oh yes, Pembers.' Churchill felt a smile spread across her face. The frustration of being found by Mr Letcher had made her briefly forget about her discovery. 'I found something very interesting indeed.'

Chapter Twenty-Two

Pemberley parked the Austin Seven Chummy Tourer in the marketplace so the two ladies could talk without shouting over the noise of the engine.

'I found some incriminating photographs, Pembers,' said Churchill. 'And you'll never guess who was in them.'

'You'd better tell me if I'll never guess.'

'Chief Inspector Llewellyn-Dalrymple,' said Churchill. 'In fact, I didn't recognise him initially because he was wearing his civvies.'

'Why has Mr Letcher got photographs of Chief Inspector Llewellyn-Dalrymple in his garage?'

'Because they're compromising photographs. There was someone else in each of the photographs, too.'

'Who?'

'Mrs Honeypear.'

'The tea room lady?'

'Yes.'

'What was she doing in the photographs with Chief Inspector Llewellyn-Dalrymple? I didn't realise they even knew each other.'

'There was a photograph of them having a picnic together by a river. And a photograph of them sitting together at a table in a restaurant. And then the most shocking photograph was of them locked in an embrace.' Churchill shuddered at the memory of it.

Pemberley gasped. 'Locked in an embrace? So they were having a love affair?'

'It seems so, Pembers. I think we can understand now why Chief Inspector Llewellyn-Dalrymple was always lenient with Mr Letcher. He had proof of his infidelity! Mr Letcher must have had him wrapped around his little finger.'

'Oh dear. Poor Mrs Llewellyn-Dalrymple. I wonder if she knew?'

'I don't think she did, Pembers. If she had, then Letcher wouldn't have been able to use the photographs as a bargaining tool, would he? He probably threatened to show the photographs to Mrs Llewellyn-Dalrymple if Chief Inspector Llewellyn-Dalrymple ever tried to prosecute him for anything.'

'Shocking.'

'So we need to speak to Mrs Honeypear now and see what she has to say about this.'

'Oh dear. She won't like us asking her questions about it.'

'No, she won't. But it has to be done.'

Pemberley drove the short distance to the tea rooms and parked the car outside. Oswald happily rested on the driver's seat while the two ladies went into the tea rooms.

They made themselves comfortable at a table by the window and Mrs Honeypear came over to take their order. 'Hello ladies! What would you like?' She wore a floral apron and a pink bow in her wavy fair hair.

They ordered tea and walnut cake.

'You didn't ask her about the affair,' Pemberley whispered when Mrs Honeypear had left again.

'I wanted to get our order in first,' said Churchill. 'I didn't want anything getting in the way of our tea and cake.'

'So you'll ask her when she comes back?'

'Yes.'

'And what if she gets upset?'

'I should think it's quite likely she'll get upset,' said Churchill. 'She was having an affair with the chief inspector, and then he was murdered. It must be very difficult for her.'

Once they'd enjoyed their tea and cake, Mrs Honeypear returned to their table and smiled. 'Was everything to your satisfaction, ladies?'

'Yes, it was lovely,' said Churchill. 'Would you join us for a moment?' She gestured to a spare chair.

'Of course.' Mrs Honeypear sat down.

'I wonder if we may ask you briefly about Chief Inspector Llewellyn-Dalrymple?'

The tea room proprietor's face paled.

'It was very sad. And I lost my favourite teapot that day. I've put in an order for a new one, but it will take time to be delivered.' She pulled a handkerchief from her apron pocket and dabbed her eyes.

'Are your tears only for your teapot, Mrs Honeypear? Or could they be for Chief Inspector Llewellyn-Dalrymple, too?'

'Well, obviously I'm upset about that as well. Everyone's upset about it, aren't they? He was the chief inspector. No one expected him to get murdered.'

'How well did you know him?' asked Churchill.

A pause followed and Mrs Honeypear bit her lip. 'You know, don't you?' she said quietly.

Churchill gave a nod. 'I'm afraid we do.'

'We loved each other.'

'I'm sorry to hear it. This must be a very difficult time for you.'

'It's awful. He was going to leave his wife, and we were going to get married.'

'I see.' It was a familiar scenario, and Churchill doubted the chief inspector would have left his wife. She didn't doubt, however, that Mrs Honeypear felt genuine sadness about his death.

'How long did your affair last?'

'Four years.'

'Four? Golly. I'm impressed no one found out.'

'We kept it very secret. Which is why I'm puzzled that you found out, Mrs Churchill.'

'I can't reveal my source.' Churchill didn't want her to know about the photographs Mr Letcher kept in his drawer. She knew how upset she would be about it. 'Please trust me, your secret is not widely known, Mrs Honeypear. However, you may know something useful to help the police investigation.'

'I can't possibly tell the police I was having an affair with their chief inspector. It would tarnish his reputation.'

'But I think it would be useful all the same, Mrs Honeypear. If the chief inspector was so worried about his reputation being tarnished, then why did he have an affair in the first place?'

'I don't know.' She dabbed her eyes again. 'It's all such a terrible mess.'

'Have you any idea who could have attacked Chief Inspector Llewellyn-Dalrymple with your teapot?'

'No. No idea at all.'

'I recall you being in the refreshments tent for the entire afternoon.'

'I was. And the only time I left it was to watch the Morris dancers, because that's what everyone else was doing at the time.'

'Did you see anyone suspicious lingering near the refreshments tent shortly before the Morris dancers struck up their dance? The murderer must have waited for you to leave the tent before they went in there and attacked Chief Inspector Llewellyn-Dalrymple.'

'I didn't see anyone suspicious. Obviously, I wish I had done, and then I could report them to the police.'

'Why do you suppose Chief Inspector Llewellyn-Dalrymple went into the tent while the Morris dancers were dancing?'

'I can only guess he went in there to speak to me while everyone else was watching the dance. And he must have just been turning around to leave and then... and then the murderer struck. Oh, it's just horrendous!'

'I appreciate you being so honest with us, Mrs Honeypear. This can't be easy for you.'

She lowered her voice to a whisper. 'You won't tell anyone, will you? It was always meant to be our secret.'

'I won't tell anyone, just as long as your affair had nothing to do with his murder.'

'It didn't!'

'Very well. Our lips are sealed for the time being. There's another matter to ask you about, too.'

'What is it?'

'Mrs Thonnings' simnel cake recipe.'

Mrs Honeypear groaned. 'I've already told Mrs Thonnings that it's my grandmother's secret recipe. That's all there is to it. I would never steal someone else's recipe.'

'Does your recipe contain, by any chance, a secret ingredient?'

'Yes, it does. It contains a secret ingredient which only my family knows about.'

'Given that both you and Mrs Thonnings know what the secret ingredients in your recipes are, it might be worth comparing your recipes. That would provide the proof the recipe wasn't stolen.'

'No! I refuse to do that! I swore to my mother and grandmother that I would never share the recipe with anyone outside our family!'

Churchill sighed. 'Well, that's a shame. Because if you could perhaps share your recipe with Mrs Thonnings—and just Mrs Thonnings—then perhaps you would be able to see if there are any similarities. And if, as you maintain, the two recipes are different, then it will stop Mrs Thonnings from accusing you of having stolen it, wouldn't it?'

'Perhaps it would, but I could never share that recipe with someone outside the family. And that's all there is to it!'

Chapter Twenty-Three

CHURCHILL AND PEMBERLEY GOT INTO THEIR CAR OUTSIDE the tea rooms and drove the short distance to their office.

'Do you think Mrs Honeypear was telling us the truth, Pembers?' asked Churchill as they climbed out of the car.

'Yes, I think so,' said Pemberley. 'It can't have been easy for her to admit to the affair with Chief Inspector Llewellyn-Dalrymple. She clearly doesn't want anybody to know about it.'

'I agree. I certainly believed that part of her account. But let's think about this for a moment. We've already considered she could be the murderer because she had the best opportunity, didn't she? The attack happened in her refreshments tent, and the weapon was her teapot. It makes sense to me that Chief Inspector Llewellyn-Dalrymple strolled into that tent while the Morris dancers were performing, and she was angry with him for some reason and smashed the teapot over his head.'

'She didn't suggest she was angry at him.'

'That's because she's not going to admit to it, is she?

Love affairs can be extremely volatile things. You know what it's like.'

'No, I don't know what it's like.'

'I'm not suggesting you have firsthand experience, Pemberley. But we know Mrs Thonnings well, and she's had a lot of these affairs. And from what she tells us, they're volatile things. Chief Inspector Llewellyn-Dalrymple had clearly promised Mrs Honeypear he was going to leave his wife so they could get married. Well, we know that's something that's commonly said in these sorts of affairs. What if she'd been pestering him for some time to leave his wife, and he was refusing to do so? Perhaps she lost her temper and hit him with the teapot.'

'Yes, that makes sense. I can imagine that happening.'

'And on the other hand, there's Mrs Llewellyn-Dalrymple to consider. We don't know whether or not she knew about her husband's affair. Perhaps she found out. And perhaps she was so enraged by the discovery that she was the one who hit him over the head with the teapot.'

Pemberley nodded. 'I'm worried we have too many suspects to consider now.'

'Don't worry, I'm about to narrow them down.' Churchill opened her handbag and pulled out a teacup which she'd wrapped in her handkerchief.

Pemberley gasped. 'You stole a teacup from the tea rooms?'

'I've borrowed it,' said Churchill. 'And I shall return it. I'll tell Mrs Honeypear it accidentally fell into my handbag.'

'I've never known that to happen before.'

'Neither have I. But it's the only excuse I can think of. Now then, let's go inside and see if we can retrieve Mrs Honeypear's fingerprints from this teacup.'

Once inside the office, Churchill took out the fingerprint testing kit and began her work. Pemberley made some tea, and a short while later, Churchill had successfully retrieved a fingerprint from the teacup. She rubbed her palms together in glee. 'It worked, Pembers!'

'How exciting!' Pemberley placed the tea tray on Churchill's desk. 'And does the fingerprint match the one you took from the teapot shard?'

'I shall check now.'

Her hands trembled with anticipation as she opened her desk drawer and took out the piece of card with the fingerprint she'd taken from the teapot shard. She then picked up her magnifying glass and closely examined the two.

Her heart flipped with excitement. 'I don't believe it, Pembers! We've got a match! Come and have a look.'

She handed the magnifying glass to Pemberley and showed her what to look for in each fingerprint.

'It matches, alright,' said Pemberley.

'There you go, you see! It was Mrs Honeypear who picked up that teapot. We've got her!'

Pemberley pulled a sceptical expression.

'What's the matter, Pembers? Why aren't you excited?'

'We would expect Mrs Honeypear's fingerprints to be on the teapot, Mrs Churchill. She was using it to serve tea all afternoon.'

Churchill's shoulders sank. 'Oh goodness. So she did. I got so carried away about the fingerprints matching that I completely forgot the teapot belonged to her in the first place.' She sat back in her chair. 'Oh, what a fool I've been, Pemberley. So the fingerprint doesn't belong to the murderer at all.'

'But it might do,' said Pemberley. 'It's still possible Mrs

Honeypear is the murderer. We just can't prove it by using the fingerprints on the teapot.'

'Yes,' said Churchill. 'You're right, Pemberley. So this fingerprint examination has got me nowhere.'

Chapter Twenty-Four

Inspector Kendall swaggered into Churchill and Pemberley's office the following morning. He took off his cap, hung it on the hatstand, and stood in the centre of the room with his hands on his hips.

'What have we done to deserve this visit, Inspector?' asked Churchill.

'I'm following up a complaint,' he said.

'What sort of complaint?'

'A complaint from a local gentleman who claims you've been harassing him.'

'Would the local gentleman be Mr Letcher, by any chance?'

'Yes, it is,' said the inspector. He grabbed a chair, span it round and sat on it back-to-front with his legs either side. 'So you know exactly what I'm referring to then, Mrs Churchill.'

'We're not harassing him, Inspector. We merely asked him a few questions.'

'There's a fine line between a few questions and harassment, Mrs Churchill.'

'The word harassment suggests we caused him some undue strain and stress. We didn't at all.'

'Only Mr Letcher can decide whether he felt strained and stressed by your questions, Mrs Churchill. And it seems to me he did.'

'Well, he's just exaggerating so he can report us to you and get us in trouble.'

'May I ask why you were asking him questions?'

'We're carrying out an investigation.'

'What sort of investigation?'

'We're trying to establish why Mr Letcher, a well-known criminal, has escaped prosecution several times. It seems Chief Inspector Llewellyn-Dalrymple had a soft spot for him.'

'Impossible. Chief Inspector Llewellyn-Dalrymple would never have a soft spot for anyone. Not even his wife.' He gave a brief chuckle. 'Sorry, that was an inappropriate comment. He did have a soft spot for his wife. Now why are you trying to find out why Letcher has supposedly evaded prosecution for alleged crimes?'

'It's an observation of ours. It seems young Fred Beanfork was wrongly imprisoned for burgling Mr Gilding's jeweller's shop. There are theories that Mr Letcher was the robber that day, and Chief Inspector Llewellyn-Dalrymple made sure Fred Beanfork was prosecuted instead of Letcher.'

Inspector Kendall let out a booming laugh. 'Absolutely impossible, Mrs Churchill! Are you questioning the integrity of a deceased chief inspector?'

'Yes, I suppose I am. And I've been rather curious about it ever since Mrs Beanfork told me her son was wrongfully imprisoned.'

'The mother of every criminal under the sun would say the same thing,' said Kendall. 'No one wants to admit their son is a criminal. It seems you've fallen for one of her fibs.'

'Well, I believe her.'

'You certainly enjoy investigating things, don't you, Mrs Churchill? It's a shame you didn't want to give me any help with my inquiries when I last called on you.'

'It's just not clear who's responsible for the police inquiries,' said Churchill. 'Is it you, or is it Inspector Mappin?'

'Inspector Mappin has retired!'

'Not according to him, he hasn't.'

'The man's a fool. I'll solve this case long before he does. Just you wait and see.'

'I think you would fare much better if you worked together, Inspector. With Mappin's knowledge of this village and your, er…' She struggled to find a word. 'Enthusiasm, let's say, you could solve the case together. Wouldn't that be wonderful?'

Kendall got up from his chair and retrieved his cap from the hat stand. 'I'd rather eat this hat than work with him, Mrs Churchill.' He planted it firmly on his head. 'Good day to you.'

'What a stubborn man,' said Churchill once he'd left the office. 'Were there any offers in the bakery this morning?'

'Four iced buns for the price of three.'

'Marvellous. How many did you buy?'

'Three.'

'Three?'

A knock sounded at the door and Mrs Thonnings stepped into the office. 'Good morning ladies! How's the investigation into my simnel cake recipe?'

'We've spoken to Miss Applethorn, Mr Greystone and Mrs Honeypear about it. But no progress, I'm afraid.'

Mrs Thonnings narrowed her eyes. 'And what did Mrs Honeypear have to say for herself?'

'She's adamant the recipe was passed down to her from her grandmother.'

'She's lying.'

'I told her that if the pair of you shared your recipes with each other, then you'd be able to directly compare—'

'No! I refuse to do that.'

Churchill sighed. 'So did she. I feel like we've reached an impasse.'

'No, we haven't. All you have to do is find out who copied it down when they were at my cottage.'

'Very well. But there are a lot of people to ask, Mrs Thonnings, and we're also busy investigating the murder of the chief inspector.'

'You need more staff, Mrs Churchill.'

'No, we don't, we shall get through this.'

'Talking of which, I was delighted to hear I'm at the top of your waiting list.'

Churchill groaned. 'Where did you hear that from?'

'Miss Applethorn. Apparently, she wants to become a private detective too, and Miss Pemberley told her there was a waiting list, and that I'm at the top of it.'

'I think there's been a slight misunderstanding, Mrs Thonnings,' said Churchill. 'It's a hypothetical waiting list.'

Mrs Thonnings frowned. 'What do you mean by that?'

'Well, there isn't actually an official waiting list. It's just that if there were a waiting list, then you would probably be first on it because you asked some time ago if you could join the detective agency.'

Mrs Thonnings looked puzzled. 'I'm confused, Mrs Churchill. You say there isn't really a waiting list, but if there were a waiting list, I would be at the top of it.'

'Yes. Exactly.'

The haberdasher's face brightened again. 'Well, it's nice to know that if there was one, I would be at the top of it.'

'Good. Would you like a cup of tea and an iced bun?'

'Yes, I would love one. And then you can tell me how you got on with my Mr Greystone.'

The ladies chatted for a while and Mrs Thonnings went on her way. Moments later, she climbed the stairs back to their office.

'Something's happened in the village,' she puffed. 'I don't know what, but everyone's heading up the high street as if they're going to look at something.'

Churchill picked up her handbag and got to her feet. 'Right then, let's see what's going on.'

Chapter Twenty-Five

CHURCHILL, PEMBERLEY, MRS THONNINGS, AND OSWALD headed outside.

'We'll take the motor car,' said Churchill. 'It's quicker.' She climbed in.

'Room for a small one?' Mrs Thonnings squeezed onto the seat beside her and Churchill found herself wedged uncomfortably between her and Pemberley. Oswald clambered onto her lap.

'I can't quite close this door,' said Mrs Thonnings. 'But it's alright, I'll just hang onto it. We're not going far, are we?'

'I hope not,' said Pemberley. 'It's so cramped in here, I've barely got the use of my arms.'

'Let's get going,' said Churchill. 'The sooner we get there, the better.'

Pemberley got the car going, and they were soon charging up the high street.

'You might want to slow down a bit, Pembers!' shouted Churchill. 'You're startling people.' She waved politely at a man who was shaking his fist at them, having just jumped out of their way.

They continued to the end of the high street to where people were turning left into a narrow lane lined with cottages.

'I wonder what can be going on?' said Mrs Thonnings.

Pemberley beeped the car horn which cleared the road but appeared to annoy several people. They crawled along the lane and eventually reached a spot where a crowd had gathered.

The three ladies and their dog clambered out of the car, keen to take a closer look.

'Good golly,' said Mrs Thonnings. 'Everyone's gathered outside Inspector Mappin's front gate.'

They squeezed their way through the crowd with Oswald in tow.

Inspector Mappin's gate was set in a low stone wall. Beyond the wall they could see into the well-tended garden surrounding the pretty beamed cottage which the inspector shared with his wife.

Beyond the garden were rolling hills of farmland. A hedge separated the farm from Inspector Mappin's garden. The hedge had a large hole torn through it. And in the centre of the garden stood a large red tractor.

'Good grief,' said Churchill. 'Someone's driven a tractor into Inspector Mappin's garden! Why?'

'Oh dear,' said Mrs Thonnings. 'Look beneath the tractor wheels. Something's lying broken there. I think it's Mappin's bench.'

'Bench?' said Churchill, her blood running cold. 'Don't tell me someone was sitting on it at the time!'

'I don't like to think of it,' said Pemberley.

'Who does the field belong to?' asked Churchill.

'It's one of Farmer Drumhead's fields,' replied Mrs

Thonnings. 'His farm is up at the top over there.' She pointed to the horizon.

'Golly,' said Churchill.

'Alright everyone,' came a voice. 'No need for all this excitement. There's nothing to see here!' Inspector Mappin stepped into view.

'Yes, there is!' came a reply from the crowd. 'You've got a ruddy great tractor in your garden.'

'Oh, thank goodness the inspector is alright,' said Churchill with relief. 'I feared the worse for a moment.'

Inspector Mappin walked over to his shed and came out again with a small crate. He placed it on his lawn in front of the tractor and stood on it.

'Can I ask for quiet, please?'

Silence fell as everyone listened to what he had to say.

'I would like to reassure you all that no one has been hurt. I can't speak for the driver—he's run off. I don't know who was behind the wheel of this tractor. But you were right to be concerned because the garden bench it crushed was the same bench I'd been sitting on just moments before the tractor came hurtling through the hedge towards me.' Gasps sounded. 'Perhaps its brakes failed,' added Mappin. 'But I managed to dive off the bench just in time before the tractor squashed it.'

A ripple of applause followed.

'Where's the driver gone?' shouted someone. 'He should be ashamed of himself!'

'Was it Farmer Drumhead?' someone else asked.

'I don't know who it was,' said Inspector Mappin. 'It all happened too quickly for me to even realise what was going on. But whoever was behind the wheel was a bit of a coward, if you ask me, because he didn't stop to check that my wife and I were unharmed. Anyway, I'll be paying a visit to Farmer Drumhead's farm shortly, and we'll get to the bottom of this. If it was something as simple as the brake system failing, then it couldn't be helped. But it's a shame the driver took off before we could establish what happened here. So there's no need for anyone to be alarmed—you may all get back to your business without worrying about anything further.'

People began to drift away, their curiosity satisfied.

'Goodness me,' said Churchill. 'Why did the tractor driver run away?'

'It's as if he didn't want his identity to be known,' said Pemberley. 'Do you think the brakes on the tractor really failed? Or do you think he drove at Inspector Mappin deliberately?'

Chapter Twenty-Six

CHURCHILL AND PEMBERLEY RETURNED TO THEIR MOTOR car. 'Let's go and speak to Fred Beanfork,' said Churchill. 'He works on Farmer Drumhead's farm and he might have seen who was driving that tractor.'

'I won't join you this time,' said Mrs Thonnings. 'I need to get on with some preparation. I've got a little plan up my sleeve.'

'What sort of plan?'

'You'll see, Mrs Churchill.' Mrs Thonnings gave her an enigmatic wink and sidled away.

The car felt spacious without Mrs Thonnings crammed into it. Churchill held onto her hat as Pemberley drove them up the hill to the farm. She stopped when they reached a bumpy track.

'We'll have to walk the rest of the way,' she said. 'The suspension on the Chummy Tourer won't cope with those lumps and bumps.'

They got out of the car and Oswald trotted ahead of them as they walked along the track. To their right, they had a good view of Compton Poppleford nestling in the valley. The sun shone and large fluffy clouds drifted lazily across the blue sky.

Churchill took her field glasses out of her handbag and focused them on the view. She could see the red tractor in the garden of Mappin's house on the edge of the village.

'Fred Beanfork could have been driving the tractor,' said Pemberley.

'Yes, he could. We know he bore a grudge against Chief Inspector Llewellyn-Dalrymple because he was wrongfully imprisoned for three years. And perhaps he bore a grudge against Inspector Mappin, too? Perhaps he's trying to wipe out the entire police force? I can understand why the young man is upset after being jailed for something he didn't do. But if he's behind this, he can't be allowed to continue. Poor Inspector Mappin—he looked quite shaken up just then. It's lucky he was able to dive out of the way in time. This could have been an attempt at murder, Pembers.'

They reached the farmhouse just as Farmer Drumhead was stepping out of the door. Oswald ran up to him and sniffed his legs. The farmer gave him a pat.

'What a terrible accident,' Churchill said to him. 'I'm relieved nobody was harmed.'

The farmer took off his cap and scratched the back of his head.

'Aye, it's just as well. Wait till I get my hands on the lad who was driving it.'

'Do you know who was driving it?'

'No. It was either Billy, Harry, or Fred.'

Churchill felt her ears prick up at the mention of Fred's name. 'But you can't be sure which of them it was?'

'No, I can't be sure. But I'll find out. There was no need for any of them to be using a tractor in that field. I'm leaving it fallow this year, so there was no call for it.'

'Can you think of any reason why they would have done it?'

'Perhaps they fancied a bit of fun, but then the brakes failed, and they ran off. I'll catch up with them sooner or later.'

'How likely do you think it is that the brakes failed, Farmer Drumhead?' asked Churchill.

'Well, it would be a surprise to me. I checked the brakes on it just last week, and everything was in working order. It's a decent tractor, that one, one of my best ones. So I'm surprised that it should have a failure like that. But that's the way with farm equipment these days—none of it's as good as it used to be.'

'Have you ever had any brakes fail on any of your tractors before?'

'No. Can't say I have. But there's a first time for everything.'

'How's the new recruit, Fred Beanfork, settling in?'

'He's doing very well, Mrs Churchill. He needed someone to give him a chance when he came out of prison, and I was happy to do so. I've known the Beanfork family for many years.'

'He maintains he was wrongly imprisoned for the robbery,' said Churchill. 'He says he didn't do it.'

'Well, it was out of character for him. But who knows with young lads? Sometimes someone puts them up to it, and they can't help themselves, can they? Anyway, as far as I'm concerned, that's all in the past now. He's started again here with a clean slate, and that's all that matters. Now, if you don't mind, I need to fetch the tractor from Mappin's garden and find out who was driving it.'

. . .

They continued along the track until they reached the field which the tractor had been driven down. By a barn nearby, they spotted pear-shaped Mrs Beanfork and her son.

'What's Mrs Beanfork doing up here?' whispered Churchill.

The mother and son stopped talking as soon as Churchill and Pemberley approached.

'Oh, hello ladies,' said Mrs Beanfork. 'Fred and I were just discussing this morning's events. I came up here to check he was alright.'

'And are you alright, Fred?' Churchill asked.

The young man nodded. 'Yes, we're all a bit surprised here, but everyone at the farm is fine.'

'It's such a relief,' said Mrs Beanfork.

'Do you know what happened?' Churchill asked Fred.

The young man shrugged. 'All I know is the tractor drove down the field, crashed through the hedge, and went into Inspector Mappin's garden. He was lucky to escape.'

'Who was driving the tractor?'

The young man shrugged again. 'I don't know. I didn't see. I was repairing the wall on the top of Barrow Hill when I saw the tractor in this field here. It just headed straight down the hill for the houses at the bottom.'

'Do you think someone did it deliberately?'

'I don't see why they would. But I also don't see why the tractor just drove down the hill like that.'

'And you have no idea who was driving it?'

'No. I think someone got onto the farm and did it deliberately.'

'Goodness,' said Churchill. 'That suggests the brakes didn't fail at all. That suggests someone came onto the farm this morning, got hold of that tractor, and drove it at Inspector Mappin's house. They must have spotted him in his garden.'

Mrs Beanfork gasped. 'They tried to murder him? Horrendous. I can't say I ever liked the man myself, but he doesn't deserve to be squashed by a tractor.'

'Why don't you like him?' Churchill asked.

'Well, he just stood by while Chief Inspector Llewellyn-Dalrymple got Fred locked up in jail. He did nothing about it! None of the police officers around here did anything to help an innocent young man. But despite all that, Inspector Mappin didn't deserve to have a tractor driven at him.'

Churchill shook her head. 'It certainly is baffling.' She turned to Fred Beanfork. 'Did you say you were up on Barrow Hill when this happened?'

The young man nodded.

'Was anyone with you?'

He shook his head. 'No, I was there by myself repairing a wall.'

'Did anyone see you there?'

'I don't know. Some sheep did, I suppose.'

'Just a moment,' said Mrs Beanfork, scowling. 'You're not suggesting my son Fred could have driven that tractor, are you, Mrs Churchill?'

'Oh no, absolutely not,' said Churchill, keen not to anger her. 'I'm just trying to establish who was where and when at the time. But I think the most likely explanation at the moment is what you've described, Fred. Someone got onto the farm and stole that tractor this morning intending to murder Inspector Mappin.'

Chapter Twenty-Seven

AFTER LEAVING MRS BEANFORK AND HER SON, CHURCHILL and Pemberley made their way to the field the tractor had been driven through.

'Let's have a look at the scene,' said Churchill.

'Look, the gate's open,' said Pemberley.

'So the tractor was driven through the gate and down the field. It's quite easy to see where because it's left its tyre tracks. Let's follow them.'

They followed the tracks through the field towards the village. Oswald scampered after a rabbit and it ducked away from him into the hedgerow.

'Now the question is, Pemberley, can the tractor attack on Inspector Mappin be connected to the murder of Chief Inspector Llewellyn-Dalrymple?'

'I think it must be,' said Pemberley. 'And despite their denials, I think Mrs Beanfork and Fred Beanfork could have something to do with this. Mrs Beanfork was seen hitting Chief Inspector Llewellyn-Dalrymple with her handbag shortly before he was murdered. We know she did this because she was angry at him for imprisoning her son.

We also know Fred Beanfork was at the retirement party that day. Either or both of them could have murdered Chief Inspector Llewellyn-Dalrymple in the refreshments tent. And then Fred Beanfork was suspiciously working on the farm where a tractor was driven deliberately at Inspector Mappin's garden. He says he was on Barrow's Hill, but we've only got his word for it. And what's Mrs Beanfork doing up here? She told us she hurried here when she heard what had happened and wanted to make sure Fred was all right. But is that true? Could she have driven the tractor at Inspector Mappin?'

'What a fair summary, Pembers,' said Churchill. 'I think whoever carried out this tractor attack bears a grudge against the police force. Both the Beanforks are extremely suspicious.' She winced as she twisted her ankle on a tussock of grass. 'Goodness, I much prefer walking on a flat and level surface. Anyway, where were we? Ah yes. The question is, Pembers, could one of the Beanforks have carried out the attack then managed to run back up to the farm before we got there?'

'Yes, I think so.'

'Someone must have seen who was running away from the tractor this morning.'

'It was a Beanfork,' said Pemberley. 'I feel sure of it. The pair of them had both the opportunity and the motive.'

'Let's think about some of our other suspects for a moment. There's Letcher to consider. We suspect he controlled Chief Inspector Llewellyn-Dalrymple because he had compromising photographs of him and Mrs Honeypear. Could he have been doing the same to Inspector Mappin?'

'Inspector Mappin has always been hapless,' said Pemberley, 'but I can't imagine anyone managing to blackmail him. As far as I'm aware, he's led a fairly sensible existence. He certainly wouldn't have had a love affair with someone.'

'Perhaps Mappin had plans to go after Letcher now that Llewellyn-Dalrymple's out of the way,' said Churchill. 'Perhaps Letcher decided Mappin needed to be taken out. It would be interesting to find out where he was at the time the tractor was driven down this hill. Although I'm not going to risk speaking to him myself again.'

'But there's also Mrs Llewellyn-Dalrymple,' said Pemberley. 'If she knew about her husband's affair, she could have murdered him in anger. Perhaps she also bore a grudge against Inspector Mappin.'

'That's an interesting thought. And let's not forget that Mrs Honeypear could have murdered Chief Inspector Llewellyn-Dalrymple too. Would she have a reason for attacking Inspector Mappin? There are still so many unanswered questions.'

They reached the bottom of the field and approached the flattened section of hedge.

'The driver of the tractor would have had a clear view of Inspector Mappin sitting on his garden bench from this field,' said Churchill. 'You'd have thought that if the brakes on the tractor had failed, then the driver would have been shouting out to Mappin to move. But we didn't hear any report of that, did we?'

Oswald skipped through the gap and into Mappin's garden. Churchill and Pemberley followed. The garden sloped gently uphill towards the house.

'Goodness me, what a mess that tractor made,' said Churchill. 'I would be furious if this was my garden.'

They walked up to the tractor, which had stopped just short of a small, paved terrace in front of Mappin's home.

'He could have driven straight into his house!' said Pemberley.

'He could have done. I think the slope of the garden slowed him somewhat, and so he could only get as far as the bench. But I suppose that was his target.'

Churchill bent down and examined the broken pieces of timber from the bench.

'Completely flattened.'

They both paced around the tractor, surveying the scene.

'I wonder which way the assailant ran off?' said Pemberley. 'I think it's unlikely he would have headed for the houses because someone might have seen him. I think he probably went back into the field and ran along the boundary. From there, he could have run back up to the farm or come out on Honeysuckle Lane, which is usually quiet.'

Churchill spotted some tulips which had been trampled in a flower bed. 'Isn't that a shame? Such lovely tulips. Oh, just a moment—look. I think we have a footprint here.'

Pemberley joined her.

'Yes, it's definitely a footprint! From a large boot.'

'I'll get my notebook out and make a sketch of it,' said Churchill. 'This is an excellent clue, Pembers. It should be easy to find the owner of this boot.'

'How do you know it's not Inspector Mappin's boot?' asked Pemberley.

'I hardly think Inspector Mappin is going to trample on his own tulips, is he?'

'Perhaps he accidentally trampled on them when he was leaping out of the way of the tractor.'

'That's a good point, Pemberley. We'll have to ask him about that just to be certain. But whoever stepped in this flower bed is likely to have muddy boots. Can we see any other footprints?'

'Not at the moment,' said Pemberley. 'But this one seems to point towards the hedge. It looks to me like someone jumped down from that tractor and ran across the flower bed to get to the hole in the hedge and then ran out that way.'

They headed back to the gap in the hedge. As they went back into the field again, they could see some patches of mud close to the hedge.

'Yes, you're right, Pemberley! There's another footprint here, and it looks the same,' said Churchill. 'We've got the culprit's footprints, alright! Please can you measure the footprint with your tape measure while I finish my sketch?'

A few minutes later, the two ladies had finished their analysis of the footprints. 'This is excellent work, Pembers,' said Churchill. 'Let's hop back into the motor car and get back to the office to work on this some more.' She glanced around. 'Where's the car?'

Pemberley glanced up the steep hill they'd just walked down. 'We parked it up at Farmer Drumhead's farm, remember?'

Chapter Twenty-Eight

Churchill had a doze at her desk when she and Pemberley finally got back to their office. She was just coming round with a cup of tea when she heard footsteps on the stairs.

Moments later, a stocky masked figure dressed in black stepped into the room.

'Ta da!'

Churchill's tea slopped into her saucer. She put down her teacup, seized her handbag, and sprang to her feet. 'Get out of here!' she yelled. 'Before we set the dog on you!'

Oswald cowered beneath Pemberley's desk. The figure pulled off their mask and ruffled their red hair.

'Don't worry, Mrs Churchill, it's only me,' said Mrs Thonnings.

Churchill fell back into her chair, clutching her chest. 'Good heavens! What on earth made you pull a stunt like that?'

'I'm sorry. I didn't realise you'd feel threatened. I expected you to laugh. I thought you'd know it was me!'

'No,' panted Churchill. 'I had absolutely no idea.'

'What do you think of my outfit? I found these slacks in my late husband's wardrobe. The black jumper was his too, and I used an old stocking for the mask.'

'Yes, it's an impressive outfit, Mrs Thonnings. But why on earth are you dressed like that?'

Mrs Thonnings pulled something out of her pocket and dangled it. 'Look what I've got.'

'A key?'

'And not just any key. It's the spare key for the tea rooms.'

'And what on earth are you doing with that?'

'I went to the tea rooms earlier and sneaked into Mrs Honeypear's office while she was serving customers. And tonight I'm going to put on this outfit, enter the tea rooms and find that simnel cake recipe.'

Mrs Churchill groaned. 'Oh dear, Mrs Thonnings, I don't think this is a good idea. What if you get caught?'

'I won't get caught. I'll be as quiet as a mouse and no one will know I'm there. I don't know why you think it's a bad idea, Mrs Churchill. After all, you do this sort of thing all the time.'

'Not all the time, Mrs Thonnings. Only when my job requires it. And besides, I'm a private detective, so it's something I'm highly experienced in. Whereas you, Mrs Thonnings...'

'What?'

'Never mind. I just don't think it's a good idea to sneak into the tea rooms. You've never done this sort of thing before.'

'I know how to sneak about, Mrs Churchill. And besides, if I asked you to do it, you would refuse.'

'What makes you say that?'

'Because you think I'm being a bit of a silly billy about

all this stolen recipe business. Well, I'm not. And I'm going to get hold of that recipe and prove that Mrs Honeypear stole it from me.'

'You're certainly very determined, Mrs Thonnings.'

'Yes, I am. And I would like to ask you a little favour, please, Mrs Churchill. Don't forget that I'm paying you to investigate this matter for me, and I think you could at least help me a little bit.'

Churchill sighed. 'What would you like me to do?'

'I'd like you to keep watch for me while I sneak into the tea rooms. And if anyone comes along, you can alert me.'

Churchill felt a sinking feeling inside. She didn't want to get involved with Mrs Thonnings sneaking into the tea rooms. But she was also worried for her friend—she didn't want her getting into trouble.

'Very well.' She turned to Pemberley. 'Perhaps you can join us on the lookout?'

'I can't this evening. Miss Applethorn and I are playing ludo.'

'Ludo? I see.' She turned back to the haberdasher. 'Very well. It looks like it will be just you and me, Mrs Thonnings.'

Chapter Twenty-Nine

Mrs Churchill met Mrs Thonnings after dark on Compton Poppleford High Street. She'd found a dark tweed skirt and a dark jacket to wear so she could melt into the shadows as she kept a lookout for Mrs Thonnings. However, she decided to try to talk her out of the plan first.

'Are you sure this is a good idea?' she asked the haberdasher. 'What will happen if you get caught?'

'Who's going to catch me?' Mrs Thonnings stared at her menacingly through the eyeholes of her stocking mask.

'Mrs Honeypear might catch you. She might return here this evening to check on something or collect something that she forgot.'

Mrs Thonnings shook her head. 'It's unlikely. And anyway, if you catch sight of her approaching, you can give a whistle and I'll know to get out. With you here, Mrs Churchill, I feel sure this plan can't go wrong.'

Churchill sighed. 'Very well. I'll do what I can to help.'

They glanced around and walked up to the tea rooms.

'Now then, Mrs Churchill. You keep an eye on everything while I open this door.'

Churchill stood in the doorway and kept watch while Mrs Thonnings unlocked the door to the tea rooms. There weren't as many shadows as she'd hoped and there was a streetlamp nearby. The shops on the other side of the street were shuttered up for the night, but there were lights on in the windows above them. Someone looking out would have a clear view of them.

'This is the riskiest part of the operation,' whispered Churchill. 'You need to get the door open quickly, Mrs Thonnings.'

'The lock's a bit stiff. There must be a knack to it.'

Churchill caught sight of movement outside the Wagon and Carrot pub. Someone had just staggered out of it. They were quite a long way down the high street, but Churchill was worried about being spotted.

'Quick,' she hissed.

She felt relieved as Mrs Thonnings got the door open and slipped inside. Churchill stepped away from the front of the tea rooms and slipped into a dark doorway close by where she could keep watch.

The person who'd emerged from the pub was staggering up the cobbled high street towards her. As he drew nearer, she saw it was Farmer Drumhead. He was humming a tune to himself.

She squeezed herself further into the doorway, pleased with her ability to hide.

'Evening, Mrs Churchill,' said the farmer, doffing his cap. He strolled on by, with little interest in what she was doing there.

Suddenly, a pool of light spilled out onto the cobbled street. Churchill startled and turned to see a light in the tea rooms had been switched on.

'Crikey, Mrs Thonnings,' she muttered under her breath.

She crept up to the tea rooms' window and peered in. She couldn't see Mrs Thonnings, but the light from the tea rooms was extremely bright. Churchill shook her head. Mrs Thonnings was drawing attention to herself. Churchill feared someone might look out of a window or suddenly appear on the street. She realised that a loud whistle, as Mrs Thonnings had planned, would merely draw more attention to the light. She realised she had to go into the tea rooms and tell Mrs Thonnings to turn off the light.

Checking no one was around, Churchill hurried into the tea rooms.

'Mrs Thonnings,' she whispered as she navigated past the tables with chairs stacked on top of them. 'Mrs Thonnings!' she whispered again as she went behind the counter and into the office.

Mrs Thonnings turned, startled, and gave out a cry.

'Shush!' said Churchill.

'What are you doing in here, Mrs Churchill? You gave me a fright!'

'You have to turn the light off! Everyone outside can see there's someone in here.'

'But I had to turn it on because I can't see anything.'

'Didn't you bring a torch with you?'

'No, I didn't think about that.'

'Then you're lucky I have one here.' Churchill pulled a torch out of her handbag.

Mrs Thonnings grinned. 'Thank you, Mrs Churchill. You've saved my life.'

'Now turn off the light.'

Mrs Thonnings did so, and they were plunged into darkness again.

'How do I turn on this torch?'

'The button's at the front. Here, let me do it.'

The Teapot Killer

After scrabbling around in the darkness, they finally managed to get the torch turned on.

'Well, seeing as you're here with me now, Mrs Churchill, you can help me look.'

'But there's no one on lookout,' said Churchill.

'I think you'll be more useful in here than out there. There's hardly anyone around, is there?'

'No. Thankfully, there isn't.' She thought of Farmer Drumhead and how he'd immediately spotted her hiding in the doorway. She reasoned that perhaps she wasn't very good at being on lookout after all, and the best she could do was help Mrs Thonnings find the recipe quickly and get out of the tea rooms.

They searched through the papers in the cupboards and on the desk.

'Where does Mrs Honeypear keep her recipes?' said Mrs Thonnings. 'She must keep them to hand.'

'In which case, perhaps they're in the kitchen,' said Churchill.

'Of course! Why didn't I think of that? Here I am checking the office. All the recipes will be kept in the kitchen.'

The two ladies made their way to the kitchen, a large room at the back with whitewashed walls and stone flags on the floor. All the pots, pans, and teapots were neatly stacked on the shelves. Churchill opened a cupboard and found rows of scrapbooks stacked inside it. She pulled one out and laid it on the counter.

'Here we are,' she said as she flipped through the book. 'Recipes.'

A handwritten recipe was pasted onto every page. Some were splattered with dried baking mixture or had extra notes scribbled on them. As Churchill leafed looked through recipes for Victoria sponge, coffee cake, lemon drizzle cake and cherry cake, her mouth began to water. Then she came across three different recipes for scones. She felt her stomach rumble.

'There's nothing I would like more now than two freshly baked scones with jam and cream.'

'Have you found the simnel cake recipe yet?' demanded Mrs Thonnings.

'Not yet. But there are more recipe books in this cupboard—why don't you take one and look through it yourself?'

The ladies spent five or ten minutes leafing through the recipe books. Churchill had to remind herself to look quickly rather than get too absorbed in the details of each one. She made a note in her mind to return to the tea rooms the following day to enjoy one of Mrs Honeypear's cakes.

'Here it is!' cried Mrs Thonnings in delight.

'Keep your voice down,' whispered Churchill. 'Someone might hear.'

'It's the same! I knew it. She copied it down from my secret recipe,' said Mrs Thonnings. She read out the list of ingredients.

'It's all listed out just the same and... yes! I don't believe it... It contains the secret ingredient!'

They heard the door of the shop open. Churchill's stomach contracted. She turned off the torch.

'Quick, hide!' she whispered.

'Where?'

'I don't know! Anywhere!'

Chapter Thirty

CHURCHILL GRABBED THE RECIPE BOOKS SHE AND MRS Thonnings had been looking at and tucked them under her arm. Then she fumbled around in the darkness of the kitchen, wondering where to go.

'Hello?' a man's voice called from the dining area. 'Is anyone in here?'

Churchill's heart pounded as she felt her way around the kitchen, desperately seeking a hiding place. She had no idea where Mrs Thonnings had gone, and there was no time to consider it either—she had to save herself. She reached out blindly for a place to hide.

Her hand fell on a door handle, and she pulled the door open with no idea where it might lead. Was it another room? Was it the water closet? She stepped forward and her foot knocked against something. Then a wooden pole hit her nose. She stifled a gasp as the pain shot through her face and made her earlobes ache.

She reached out and grabbed the item which had hit her. It felt like a broom handle.

Churchill felt sure she'd stepped into the broom

cupboard and it was a good hiding place if no one looked in it. She squeezed herself in among the buckets, boxes, and clutter making as little noise as possible. Finally, she could pull the door closed behind her. She stood there in the darkness, her chest heaving with exertion and her heart pounding. She prayed nobody would open the door.

Light spilled in beneath the door as the kitchen light was turned on.

'Hello?' came the voice again.

Churchill's knees felt weak. If she was discovered here in the cupboard, she would have a lot of explaining to do. Where had Mrs Thonnings gone? She couldn't imagine her finding a hiding place as good as the broom cupboard. She expected the haberdasher to be found at any moment. She held her breath.

'There doesn't appear to be anyone here, Mrs Honeypear,' said the man.

'Well, that is strange, Constable,' said the tea room owner's voice. 'Mrs Bentley across the road said there was definitely a light on in the tea rooms. She telephoned me as soon as she saw it.'

'Well, whoever it was appears to have scarpered,' said the constable. 'It appears you left your door unlocked, Mrs Honeypear.'

'I'm sure I locked it this evening. I don't understand it. I've never once left that door unlocked. Silly me.'

'And you're sure nothing's been taken?'

'I'll have another look in the office. But the safe is locked, and everything seems in order.'

'Mysterious indeed. Well, I'm happy to stay here as long as you like, so you can be sure that there's no one here.'

'Thank you, Constable.'

Churchill willed him to go away, but the kitchen light

remained on. For the next ten minutes or so, she heard footsteps and conversation as Mrs Honeypear and the constable looked around the premises. She doubted Mrs Thonnings would last much longer. Surely they would find her soon?

But as time passed, it seemed apparent they weren't going to.

The pair returned to the kitchen.

'Well, I suppose it was just an opportunist,' said Mrs Honeypear. 'There's no one here and nothing appears to have been taken.'

'I'm pleased to hear it. However, I can stay here and keep watch on these premises for the next hour or two,' said the constable. 'If anyone's hiding, they'll probably emerge when they think the coast is clear, and I'll catch them then.'

Churchill felt her stomach knot. Her legs already ached from standing in the broom cupboard. How were they going to cope for the next hour or two? There wasn't enough room to sit down. Her heart pounded in her ears and she dared not move a muscle in case she knocked against something and made a noise.

She closed her eyes and prayed the constable would grow bored and leave.

Chapter Thirty-One

'You look exhausted today, Mrs Churchill,' said Pemberley as Churchill arrived at the office the following morning. Her head ached, and she felt irritable.

'That's because I am tired, Pemberley. I don't suppose you picked up anything tasty from the bakery on your way here, did you?'

'Yes, half a dozen Eccles cakes.'

'Perfect.' Churchill sank into her chair. 'I shall eat them all now.'

'So what happened? Did Mrs Thonnings find the recipe?'

'Yes, she did. She read it and said it was exactly the same as her own recipe. So it seems that someone somehow copied down her recipe and gave it to Mrs Honeypear. I suppose we just have to work out who that person was.'

'So why are you so tired?'

'Because I spent much of the night standing in a broom cupboard in Mrs Honeypear's kitchen,' said

Churchill. 'A constable remained there until the small hours, and I wasn't able to escape until just before dawn.'

'Oh dear,' said Pemberley. 'That doesn't sound fun at all. And what happened to Mrs Thonnings?'

'I've no idea. I haven't seen her since Mrs Honeypear and the constable turned up at the tea rooms. But they didn't catch her, so I don't know where she hid.'

A knock sounded at the door and Mrs Thonnings stepped into the office. Her hair was bright and bouncy, and she looked well-rested. She greeted them both cheerily.

'Oh dear, Mrs Churchill, you don't look very well.'

'I don't feel very well. I only got two hours of sleep last night. What happened to you, Mrs Thonnings? Where did you hide?'

'Oh, I was very sneaky. I gave Mrs Honeypear and the constable the slip.'

'How on earth did you manage that?'

'I hid behind the kitchen door and when they turned the light on, I thought I was for it. But they were both facing away from me, looking around the room, so I sneaked out from behind the door, tiptoed through the tea rooms, and left that way. I got home just after half past ten.'

'Half past ten?' Churchill felt consumed with resentment. 'I was stuck in that broom cupboard until four o'clock, Mrs Thonnings!'

'Oh dear, that's quite a long time. I suppose I was very stealthy, Mrs Churchill.' She sat down. 'I'm very pleased last night's operation all went to plan. I was able to find the simnel cake recipe and confirm that it has indeed been stolen.'

'What are you going to do now?' asked Pemberley.

'Confront Mrs Honeypear, of course!'

'But then she'll know it was you sneaking around in the tea rooms last night.'

The haberdasher's face fell. 'I hadn't thought of that. She's going to ask how I know the recipe was stolen, isn't she? And if I tell her I saw the recipe in her book, then she'll know what I got up to. Right, I shall have to think about that. But I already feel that I am on the path to justice. I shall find a way to make sure she can never serve another slice of my simnel cake ever again. Thank you for your help, Mrs Churchill.' She reached into her purse and took out some money, placing it on Churchill's desk. 'I couldn't have done it without you.'

'I'm pleased I could be of assistance,' said Churchill with a yawn.

Chapter Thirty-Two

CHURCHILL AND PEMBERLEY DROVE TO THE POLICE STATION later that morning. Inside, the two inspectors' desks sat cheek by jowl.

'How are you feeling, Inspector Mappin, after yesterday's incident?' asked Churchill.

'I'm feeling absolutely fine, thank you, Mrs Churchill. I'm busy finding the miscreant who drove the tractor at me.'

'I haven't noticed you being busy,' said Inspector Kendall. 'You've been sitting there drinking tea and eating biscuits.'

'The tea and biscuits are fuelling my mind, Kendall,' said Mappin. 'I'll soon catch the person who did this. You wait and see.'

'Have you any ideas at the moment, Inspector?' Churchill asked.

'Not just at the moment.'

'Perhaps we could share some of our ideas?'

'There's no need for you to be getting involved in this, Mrs Churchill,' said Mappin. 'Everything is in hand.'

'Are you sure?' said Churchill. 'It's not going to be easy for you to find the person who tried to murder you.'

'Murder me?' His jaw dropped. 'No one tried to murder me!'

'But they drove a tractor at you,' said Churchill. 'What else do you think they were trying to do?'

'Probably frighten me, I expect. If I hadn't moved out of the way, then I think they would have stopped.'

Kendall gave a laugh. 'I'm not a tractor driver myself, but I can't imagine it's easy to stop a great machine like that once it's rolling down a hill.'

'Even so, I refuse to believe this was an attempt to murder me,' said Mappin. 'Why would anyone want to murder me?'

Inspector Kendall rolled his eyes and said nothing.

'Did the driver of the tractor try to warn you at any point that the brakes had failed?' asked Churchill.

'No. Nothing at all. He was quite far away, and the engine was noisy. I suppose he could have waved at me to warn me. But there was nothing of the sort. In fact, he was leaning over the steering wheel as if urging the tractor to move even faster.'

'Then there's no doubt in my mind that this attack was deliberate, Inspector. Would you recognise the driver if you saw him again?'

'I don't know. He was wearing a cap and driving goggles. And he had a scarf covering the lower part of his face. In fact, when I think about it… he was hiding his features, wasn't he?'

'It sounds very much like it,' said Churchill. 'Miss Pemberley and I are wondering if there's someone in the village who wishes to attack police officers. First Chief Inspector Llewellyn-Dalrymple, and now you, Inspector Mappin.'

'Really? You think the same person could be behind both attacks?'

'I'm afraid so. And one suspect comes to mind.'

'And who's that?'

'Young Fred Beanfork. The chap who was wrongly imprisoned for robbing Mr Gilding's jeweller's shop.'

'He wasn't wrongly imprisoned,' said Mappin. 'Chief Inspector Llewellyn-Dalrymple was adamant all the evidence pointed to him.'

'Yes, but did all the evidence actually point to Fred Beanfork? We have reason to believe that Llewellyn-Dalrymple's actions were being controlled by Mr Letcher.'

'No. Never. Chief Inspector Llewellyn-Dalrymple and I did not always see eye to eye, but there's no chance he would have had his work influenced by a known criminal.'

'You've mentioned yourself, Inspector Mappin, that Llewellyn-Dalrymple was quite lenient on Mr Letcher.'

'Yes, he was. But that was just my opinion. Anyway, I don't see why Beanfork would drive a tractor at me.'

'Because he perhaps mistakenly believed that you supported Chief Inspector Llewellyn-Dalrymple's decision to make him take the blame for the robbery at the jewellers.'

'Really? I think that's a bit of a stretch.'

'Or his mother drove the tractor.'

Inspector Kendall let out a laugh. 'Fred Beanfork's mother? You think she drove the tractor?'

Churchill shot him a sharp stare. 'All possibilities must be considered, Inspector Kendall. Surely you know that yourself?'

'All realistic possibilities. Not silly, pie-in-the-sky ideas. Now I'm sure Inspector Mappin wants to get on and make his next cup of tea. You two ladies are wasting his time.'

'Is that so?' Churchill put her hands on her hips. 'And

what have you contributed to the investigation, Inspector Kendall?'

'Quite a lot. But it would be quite wrong of me to share the details of my investigation with two old ladies.'

'Two old ladies? You asked for our help recently, Inspector.'

His face coloured. 'I did not,' he said indignantly.

'You asked Mrs Churchill and Miss Pemberley for help?' asked Mappin.

'I visited them as part of my routine inquiries to find people with local knowledge.'

'Well, you could always ask me, Kendall.'

'You're supposed to be retired.'

'And you're not even supposed to be here.'

'Inspector Mappin,' said Churchill. 'Did you trample on your tulips while escaping the tractor's path?'

'I really can't recall. All I know is I saw the vehicle heading straight towards me, and I leapt out of the way. I didn't have the chance to check for tulips or anything else, for that matter.'

'Are you aware there's a large footprint in your tulip flower bed?'

'Is there indeed? Well, it's possible it could be mine. But I shall have a look at it and see.'

'There was also a similar footprint in the field on the other side of the hedge,' said Churchill. 'Miss Pemberley and I believe both footprints could belong to the culprit who quickly made his getaway from the tractor.'

'Is that so? Right then, I shall have a look as soon as I get home. Although I may have trampled my tulips, I certainly didn't run out into the field. So I shall examine those footprints and determine whether they're mine or not. Thank you for pointing them out to me, Mrs Churchill. I must admit this whole affair has shaken me up quite a bit, and I hadn't really given much thought to examining the garden for footprints. But it makes an enormous amount of sense. After all, the chap got away.'

Churchill, Pemberley and Oswald left the police station and began walking back to their office. They had walked twenty yards when Pemberley stopped. 'Just a moment,' she said. 'We drove here, didn't we?'

'Oh yes. Silly us.'

Churchill turned around to return to the motor car.

But it wasn't there.

'Are you sure we drove here, Pemberley?'

'Yes. I have the car keys in my handbag.'

'So where's the car?'

They hurried back to the spot where they'd parked it.

Churchill's head felt muddled. 'We're not confused, are we, Pemberley? We definitely arrived here in the car, didn't we?'

'Yes. We drove here, and we parked it outside the police station.'

'The road is flat. It couldn't possibly have rolled away.'

'Oh gosh,' said Pemberley. 'Someone's taken it!'

'Impossible,' said Churchill. 'There has to be another explanation.'

'There is no other explanation,' said Pemberley. 'While we were inside the police station, someone came along and stole my cousin Bertie's Chummy Tourer.'

Churchill's heart sank. 'How brazen! Why on earth would someone do something like that? And right outside a police station, too. Well, they can't have got far. Let's report it to Inspector Mappin.'

Chapter Thirty-Three

Churchill, Pemberley and Oswald spent the next few hours walking around the village looking for the missing motor car.

'Cousin Bertie is going to be so angry with me!' wailed Pemberley as they returned to the high street.

'It's not your fault, Pembers. And we parked it outside a police station. That should be the safest part of the village! Who knew that Compton Poppleford had such brazen car thieves? And besides, I'm sure your cousin Bertie can recover the cost with his insurance policy.'

'Cousin Bertie doesn't believe in things like insurance, Mrs Churchill.'

'Doesn't he? Oh dear.'

Pemberley's lower lip wobbled. 'He's going to expect me to pay for it. I just know it!'

Churchill rested a comforting hand on her shoulder. 'Now, now, Pembers, that really wouldn't be fair at all. He can't make you pay for something that wasn't your fault. I'm sure his car will turn up somewhere. Just don't tell him it's missing yet, and we'll keep looking. Fingers crossed, we'll find it before long. It can't have gone far.'

'Someone could have taken it and driven it to the other side of Dorset by now!'

'But they might not have. Let's remain hopeful. What's that noise, Pemberley? It sounds like someone shouting.'

They continued down the high street and the shouting grew louder. 'It sounds like a woman,' said Churchill. 'Perhaps it's one of those religious ladies telling everyone they're going to go to hell.'

'I don't like those ladies,' said Pemberley.

They continued on their way and saw a small group of people by the tea rooms.

'The palaver seems to be coming from the tea rooms, Pemberley.' Then Churchill stopped. 'Oh no, that's not who I think it is, is it?' She could see someone with red hair.

When they reached the tea rooms, they saw Mrs Thonnings standing outside with a large sign in her hand. It read: "Mrs Honeypear is a thief."

'Whatever you do, don't go into the tea rooms!' shouted Mrs Thonnings to the people walking past. 'Mrs Honeypear steals other people's recipes and pretends they're her own!'

She caught sight of Churchill and Pemberley. 'Oh hello, ladies. Actually, it's nicer to speak quietly for a moment—my throat is getting rather sore, and I've only been here five minutes.'

'Do you really think this is a good idea, Mrs Thonnings?'

'Of course it is. Mrs Honeypear stole my recipe, and everyone needs to know that. No one should be going into her tea rooms and spending money in there. Oi!' She turned to an elderly man who was just about to step in through the tea room door. 'Where do you think you're going?'

'I'd like to get a cup of tea,' he said.

'No, you don't! You can wait until you get home and make one then.'

'Why?'

'Because Mrs Honeypear steals other people's cake recipes. She doesn't deserve any customers.'

'I'm not after any cake. I just want a cup of tea.'

'No, you don't. Shoo!'

The elderly man pulled a frightened grimace and left.

'You've just scared away one of Mrs Honeypear's customers, Mrs Thonnings,' said Churchill.

'Good! She doesn't deserve to have any.'

The door opened, and Mrs Honeypear stepped out. 'What on earth is going on out here?' she asked. Then she saw the sign. 'I'm not a thief!'

'Yes, you are,' said Mrs Thonnings. 'You stole my simnel cake recipe.'

'I didn't!'

'Yes, you did. I know you did. You asked someone in the Ladies' Sewing Circle to have a look at the recipe and copy it out when they visited my cottage.'

Mrs Honeypear's eyes grew wide. 'I'm sorry? I don't even know anyone who's a member of the Ladies' Sewing Circle.'

'Oh yes, you do. You know most of them. And one of them copied out the recipe and gave it to you.'

'That's nonsense, Mrs Thonnings. I've already discussed this with you. That recipe was handed to me by my late grandmother. It's been in the family for generations.'

'You're lying!'

Churchill decided to intervene. 'Mrs Thonnings,' she

said, 'I really don't think this is the best course of action. Although I can understand you're upset—'

'Yes, I am upset! She stole my recipe!'

'All the time you're standing out here with your sign, you're missing out on business of your own, Mrs Thonnings. Presumably, you've had to close your own shop in order to stand here?'

'Yes, I have! And I will stop at nothing to make sure justice is served!'

'I really don't think this is justice being served, Mrs Thonnings,' said Churchill. 'I don't think people like being shouted at. Behaving like this is only going to encourage people to take Mrs Honeypear's side.'

Mrs Thonnings lowered her sign. 'Do you think so?'

'I know so. I've been looking at the faces of people passing by and they're not impressed. The residents of Compton Poppleford don't really like loud, shouting people. Surely you know that, Mrs Thonnings?'

The haberdasher gazed sadly at Mrs Honeypear. 'So how do I get my revenge?'

'I'm not sure,' said Churchill. 'Is there even any need for revenge?'

'Yes, there is!'

'I see.' Churchill took her arm. 'This case is very puzzling indeed, but I feel determined to stop you embarrassing yourself. I shall look into this further, but let's take you back to your shop first.'

Chapter Thirty-Four

'I'M GETTING RATHER WORRIED ABOUT MRS THONNINGS,' Churchill said to Pemberley once they'd escorted the haberdasher back to her shop. 'She's got very upset about this simnel cake recipe, and now she's closing her shop while she publicly embarrasses herself. It's very concerning but I have an idea and I think we can ask your friend Miss Applethorn to help.'

Pemberley's face lit up. 'Oh, Miss Applethorn would love to help!'

'Good. Then let's visit the library.'

Inside the library, Oswald scampered off to play with Whisker. Miss Applethorn was sitting behind the librarian's desk and greeted them with a warm smile. 'Hello ladies, what are you looking for today?'

'We need to look at all the village records you have here in the library, Miss Applethorn,' said Churchill. 'Anything with details of old families here in Compton Poppleford. And I also need to look at the parish register.'

'You'll find that at the church,' said Miss Applethorn,

getting to her feet. 'But in the meantime, I can certainly get out all the records we have here.'

'Thank you,' said Churchill. 'And if you have some time to spare, Miss Applethorn, I'd be very grateful if you're able to help us.'

'Really? Of course I have some spare time. I'd love to help!'

A couple of hours later, Churchill and Pemberley left the library and made their way to St Swithun's church.

'I think we're getting closer to helping Mrs Thonnings now,' said Churchill.

'Yes, we are,' said Pemberley. 'Hopefully, the conundrum will soon be sorted.'

The vicar greeted them at the church. 'How lovely to see you both,' he said. 'I don't believe I've seen either of you recently at morning service.'

'No.' Churchill scratched her nose, trying to come up with an excuse. 'Sunday mornings have been quite busy recently.'

'Oh yes. It's often the way with modern life, isn't it? But don't forget, it's important to take a break from the bustle of everyday life and find a moment for reflection. After all, the Lord did mark Sunday as a day of rest.'

'Well, yes, he did. But it seems that Sunday is the only day when I can get a bit of dusting and cleaning done. Perhaps the Lord would like to do that for me?' asked Churchill with a smile.

The vicar's expression remained impassive.

'I apologise,' said Churchill. 'It was just a little joke. I shall try to make more of an effort this coming Sunday, Vicar. In the meantime, I wonder if Miss Pemberley and I may examine your parish register?'

'Of course.'

Churchill and Pemberley left the church a short while later with a skip in their step.

'I do believe we've cracked it, Pembers,' said Churchill. 'Let's pay Mrs Thonnings a visit now and put her out of her misery.'

They found the haberdasher behind the counter of her shop with a deep frown.

'Oh goodness, Mrs Thonnings,' said Churchill. 'Cheer up, you're driving your customers away.'

'What customers?' she replied, gesturing at the empty shop.

'Exactly. You've already frightened them away. Anyway, I have some news to cheer you up.'

'Has Mrs Honeypear finally admitted to stealing my recipe? Is she going to leave Compton Poppleford with her tail between her legs?'

'No, I'm afraid not,' said Churchill. 'In fact, I remain quite convinced that Mrs Honeypear's recipe for simnel cake was passed down to her from her grandmother.'

'No! That's impossible!' said Mrs Thonnings, thumping her counter. 'How can we both have an identical recipe passed down to us by our grandmothers?'

'The answer is quite simple,' said Churchill. 'You share the same grandmother.'

Mrs Thonnings's mouth dropped open, and she stumbled on her feet. Pemberley dashed behind the counter to help steady her.

'The same grandmother? That's impossible!'

'It's not. Miss Pemberley and I have just spent several hours examining all the local records in Compton Popple-

The Teapot Killer

ford. We've examined your family tree and Mrs Honeypear's family tree.'

'It's all in the records?'

'If you know where to look, yes. Miss Applethorn, the librarian, helped us too. We've established that both you and Mrs Honeypear share the same grandmother. Mrs Hannah Cloverhawk.'

'So that means Mrs Honeypear is my... auntie?'

'Cousin, Mrs Thonnings.'

'Cousin? No, I refuse to believe it. I never encountered her during my childhood.'

'Her father and your father were brothers,' said Churchill.

'Uncle Archibald was her father?'

Churchill nodded. 'Yes, that's right.'

'But I never met her! Just a moment...' Mrs Thonnings put her finger to her lips as she thought.

'Mrs Honeypear is quite a lot younger than you,' said Churchill.

'Quite a lot younger? What do you mean?'

'She's eighteen years younger than you.'

'She looks older.'

'You were eighteen years old when she was born.'

'And when I was eighteen, I was working as a sewing mistress for a school on the other side of Dorchester,' said Mrs Thonnings. 'So I wasn't living in Compton Poppleford at the time.'

'Were you close to your Uncle Archibald?'

'Not really. He and Aunt Beth had lots of children.'

'They did indeed. Mrs Honeypear was the youngest of nine.'

'Yes, that makes sense now. There were so many of them. Mrs Honeypear was only a baby when I was eighteen, so I suppose I paid little attention to her. And I didn't return to the village until I got married. Uncle Archibald and my father were never close, and I didn't really keep up with my cousins. I quite liked the eldest one, Maggie. She eloped to France with a circus performer. Oh wait a minute, that means Mrs Honeypear is little Milly! I remember now.'

'Little Milly?' asked Churchill.

'Yes, I remember seeing her once or twice as a baby. And to think that little Milly grew up to own the tea rooms! Well, I never. There's not much of a family resemblance between us, is there? We always said, when we were growing up, that my father's side of the family had the looks.'

'Did you indeed?' said Churchill. 'Well, why don't we pay a visit to your cousin now and settle the matter once and for all?'

Their reception at the tea rooms was frosty.

'You're not allowed in here,' said Mrs Honeypear as soon as she caught sight of Mrs Thonnings.

'I'm sorry. I've come here to explain everything.'

'I can't see what there is to explain.'

'There's a lot to explain, Mrs Honeypear. Or perhaps I should call you what I remember calling you all those years ago. Little Milly.'

Mrs Honeypear froze. 'How do you know my name?'

'Because I'm your cousin. I don't think you remember me. I'd left Compton Poppleford when you were born, and I didn't come back until I got married. We weren't a close family, were we? But we have the same recipe because we have the same grandmother.'

Mrs Honeypear gasped and clasped her hands to her

face. 'Oh goodness. So that explains it! Grandma Cloverhawk passed down the simnel cake recipe to all of us!'

Mrs Thonnings gave a tearful nod. 'She did indeed. So I'm very sorry for being so obnoxious.'

'And I'm sorry for being so rude too,' said Mrs Honeypear. She pulled out her handkerchief and wiped her eyes. Mrs Thonnings did the same. As did Churchill.

'I've actually just baked another simnel cake today,' said Mrs Honeypear. 'Would you care for a slice, Mrs Thonnings?'

'I'd love to. Thank you. No simnel cake beats Grandma Cloverhawk's recipe.'

Chapter Thirty-Five

CHURCHILL AND PEMBERLEY ARRIVED BACK AT THEIR office to find Mr Greystone, the undertaker, waiting for them by their door.

'We're so sorry to have kept you waiting,' said Churchill. 'Have you been here long?'

'About forty-five minutes.'

'Oh, my goodness!'

'It's nothing when compared with the eternal sleep which awaits us all at the end of our lives.'

Churchill shivered. 'Do come and join us for a cup of tea.'

She unlocked the door, and they climbed the stairs to their office.

Once inside, Pemberley made some tea, and they all made themselves comfortable. 'I thought you might like to know something interesting,' said Mr Greystone. 'Ever since you carried out surveillance on Letcher across the road from me, I've been keeping an eye on him myself.'

'Have you indeed? That's very helpful of you,' said Churchill.

'I've noticed he has a regular visitor. For some reason, the recently widowed Mrs Llewellyn-Dalrymple keeps turning up at his garage in the evening.'

'Does she?' said Churchill. 'So the time I saw her there wasn't a singular occurrence.'

'No. It's a regular occurrence. It seems a bit odd to me that the recently widowed wife of a chief inspector should be spending time with the village crook.'

'You're right, Mr Greystone. It does seem odd. And I'm very grateful to you for letting us know. I'd like to see this for myself. Do you mind if we carry out some more surveillance at your premises this evening?'

'Not at all, Mrs Churchill.'

Once the sun had set that evening, Churchill, Pemberley and Oswald positioned themselves at the upstairs window of Mr Greystone's funeral parlour.

'There's a nice bag of pillows here,' said Pemberley. 'I've put one on my seat and now it's a lot more comfortable.'

'A pillow?'

'Yes. There are lots of them. All covered in satin too. Or is it silk? I can't tell sometimes.'

A chill ran down Churchill's spine. 'They must be coffin pillows, Pembers!'

'Well, they're very comfy. Would you like one?'

'No, thank you.' Churchill gave a shudder and hoped they didn't have to wait too long until Mrs Llewellyn-Dalrymple arrived at Letcher's Garage.

Churchill focused her field glasses on the garage. 'I see Letcher's got a few new motor cars for sale,' she said. 'He's even got an Austin Seven Chummy Tourer like Cousin Bertie's.'

'Where?' said Pemberley. 'Perhaps we could buy it from Mr Letcher and pretend to Bertie that his car never went missing.'

'If we did that, we'd have to pretend we repainted it. The one I can see is an orangey red colour.'

'I don't think Bertie would like orangey red.'

They sipped their tea, continuing to look out of the window. Before long, a sweep of car headlights illuminated the road surface.

'She's here!' said Churchill excitedly.

They peered through their field glasses, watching as Mrs Llewellyn-Dalrymple climbed out of her motor car and stepped into Mr Letcher's garage.

'Come along, Pembers. It's time to confront the pair of them.'

'Confront?' Pemberley lowered her field glasses. 'You didn't mention anything about confronting this evening, Mrs Churchill. I hate confrontations!'

'So do I, but it has to be done. I'm tired of second guessing everyone and I want to find out once and for all what's going on.'

They went downstairs and stepped outside. They crossed the road to the garage forecourt. Churchill paused by the Chummy Tourer.

'It looks very similar to Cousin Bertie's car, doesn't it? Exactly the same, except for the colour.'

'It's got different number plates,' said Pemberley.

'Oh, of course,' said Churchill. 'That's what you'd expect.'

'Just a moment,' said Pemberley, stepping closer to the car. She took her torch out of her handbag, switched it on, and shone it through the driver's window. 'It's Bertie's car!'

'What do you mean?'

'This is Bertie's car! Letcher has repainted it and put

different number plates on it. But it's exactly the same car. It's got the same rip in the driver's seat.'

'Let me have a look.' Churchill shone her own torch through the window. 'You're right, Pemberley. It is the same car. Letcher stole cousin Bertie's car from outside the police station! And now he's trying to sell it for himself!' Anger rose inside her. 'I need to have a word with Letcher about this!'

'Wait.' Pemberley rested her hand on Churchill's arm. 'You can't march in there and lose your temper with him, Mrs Churchill. It'll ruin everything. Remember why we're here. We're going to speak to Mrs Llewellyn-Dalrymple. So let's keep calm and speak to her first, and then you can confront him about the car.'

Churchill took in a breath and exhaled loudly through her nose.

'Very sensible, Pemberley. Thank you for calming me down. You're right—I was about to march into the garage shouting at him, and that would've got us nowhere. At least we've found where cousin Bertie's Chummy Tourer got to. And for now we should deal with Mrs Llewellyn-Dalrymple.'

They approached the garage and stepped inside. Mr Letcher and Mrs Llewellyn-Dalrymple were sitting at the workbench with a drink in hand and sharing a joke. Their faces turned stern as soon as they spotted the two ladies. Oswald cowered behind Pemberley's skirts.

Mr Letcher got to his feet. 'I thought I told you not to come back here, Mrs Churchill.'

'Yes, you did. But we're here to speak to Mrs Llewellyn-Dalrymple.'

'I see,' said Mrs Llewellyn-Dalrymple. 'And what can I possibly help you with?'

'We'd like to know why you're here.'

'Well, that's an impertinent question, Mrs Churchill. And it's absolutely none of your business.' She wrinkled her upturned nose.

'No, it may not be,' said Churchill. 'But you're recently widowed, Mrs Llewellyn-Dalrymple, and your late husband was the chief inspector. And yet here you are, regularly visiting a man who is a member of the criminal class. I'm afraid people are beginning to talk.'

She pursed her lips. 'Well, it has nothing to do with them.'

'What do you mean, Mrs Churchill?' said Letcher. 'A member of the criminal class? What are you accusing me of?'

'Many things, Mr Letcher. I've heard all sorts of tales about you. But I also know that you've stolen our car, repainted it, put another number plate on it, and are now trying to sell it.'

He gave a laugh. 'What nonsense. You can't prove it.'

'Oh yes, we can—and we will, Mr Letcher.' Churchill turned back to Mrs Llewellyn-Dalrymple. 'You're doing yourself a great disservice, fraternising with this man.'

'He was a friend of my late husband's,' said Mrs Llewellyn-Dalrymple.

'Are you sure he was a friend?' said Churchill. 'There's no doubt that Chief Inspector Llewellyn-Dalrymple turned a blind eye to Mr Letcher's activities. But was that because of friendship? Or was it because of something else?'

'I don't know what you're talking about,' said Mrs Llewellyn-Dalrymple.

'Perhaps you don't. But Mr Letcher knows full well what I'm talking about,' said Churchill, 'especially if I mention the photographs.'

His face grew twisted. 'I knew it, Mrs Churchill. You were in here two days ago snooping about when you claimed to be using the lavatory. You had no right to be going through my belongings.'

'What photographs?' asked Mrs Llewellyn-Dalrymple, wide-eyed.

'They're nothing,' said Mr Letcher.

'They're not nothing, Mr Letcher, because your mood has changed quite dramatically. Clearly, Mrs Churchill found some photographs among your belongings. What are they of?'

'You don't need to know. It would only upset you.'

'But I'm afraid you have to tell me, Mr Letcher,' said Mrs Llewellyn-Dalrymple, getting to her feet. 'And I shall insist on it until you do.'

He turned to her. 'Alright then. I shall tell you. But when you get upset, you need to blame her, not me.' He pointed his oil-stained finger at Mrs Churchill.

'Very well,' said Mrs Llewellyn-Dalrymple. 'I shall. Now, what are the photographs?'

'I had some photographs taken of your husband, Mrs Llewellyn-Dalrymple. Without his knowledge.'

'Why?'

He shuffled from one foot to the other. 'It was a bit of insurance.'

'I don't understand. Can you please explain it to me clearly?'

'Insurance to keep me covered. So he would leave me alone.'

'You're still doing a terrible job of explaining it, Mr Letcher.'

'Alright then. I shall say it plainly. I had some photographs taken of your husband and Mrs Honeypear together. They were having a love affair. And I had evidence of it. I told him that if he ever arrested me for anything, then I would show the photographs to you, Mrs Llewellyn-Dalrymple.'

Chapter Thirty-Six

Mrs Llewellyn-Dalrymple sighed, then sank back into her chair. 'Is that all?'

'Yes. So you can get upset at her.' Mr Letcher pointed his finger at Churchill again. 'She's the one who mentioned the photographs.'

'There's no need for me to get upset at anyone,' said Mrs Llewellyn-Dalrymple. 'It was quite obvious my husband was having an affair with Mrs Honeypear. I knew about it for months.'

Mr Letcher's shoulders slumped. 'You knew?'

'Of course I knew.'

'Did your husband know you knew?'

'Of course he didn't.'

'I see.' He ran a hand over his wavy grey hair. 'I had no idea you knew.'

'Oh yes. It was quite obvious. There he was, sneaking about, thinking I hadn't a clue. But I had. She wasn't the first mistress, and I'm sure she wouldn't have been the last if he'd lived.'

Churchill felt relieved that Mrs Llewellyn-Dalrymple

already knew about the affair—it meant she wasn't going to get upset at anyone. 'Well, that's that sorted, then,' she said. 'It seems the photographs are old news. But the fact that you possessed them, Mr Letcher, demonstrates that you were up to no good and wanted protection from prosecution.'

'No, it doesn't. And I can get rid of them now because they're no longer needed, anyway. To be honest with you, I'd quite forgotten about them until you found them, Mrs Churchill.'

'So the question remains,' said Churchill, 'why are you friends with this man, Mrs Llewellyn-Dalrymple? He was blackmailing your husband, and he's clearly a criminal despite his denials.'

'I'm friends with Mr Letcher because I like him,' said Mrs Llewellyn-Dalrymple, 'and that's all there is to it.'

Churchill shook her head in dismay. 'I struggle to believe it,' she said. 'There must be something you're not telling me.'

Mr Letcher cleared his throat. 'Perhaps there's an opportunity here to come to a little arrangement, Mrs Churchill. How about I repaint the car and put the old number plate back on it, and you don't mention any of this to Mappin or Kendall or whoever's in charge these days.'

'I don't do deals with criminals,' said Churchill. 'And I'm not finished with the pair of you. There's something you're not telling me, but I'll get to the bottom of it. You wait and see.'

Churchill and Pemberley returned to their office for a late-night cup of tea.

'So, Mrs Llewellyn-Dalrymple knew about her husband's infidelities all along,' said Churchill. 'And I suppose we shouldn't be surprised. I would have known immediately if Chief Inspector Churchill had ever strayed.'

'If Mrs Llewellyn-Dalrymple knew about her husband's affair with Mrs Honeypear, then that gives her a good motive for murdering him,' said Pemberley. 'She could have murdered him out of anger.'

'She could have. Although, from what she said, it seems she was quite used to his infidelities.'

'Perhaps she told us that because she wanted to appear unbothered by it,' said Pemberley. 'If she was angry and enraged about it, then that strengthens her motive for murdering him.'

'What an excellent point, Pembers! Of course, it does. By telling us she wasn't bothered at all, that supposedly removes her motive for murdering him. But what if it was quite the opposite? Perhaps it was the only affair she ever found out about? And perhaps, when she found out, she was so angry that she hit him over the head with his mistress's teapot. That makes sense, Pembers. Can you recall seeing her watching the Morris dancers?'

'No, I can't,' said Pemberley.

'There's little doubt that Mrs Llewellyn-Dalrymple is an extremely strong suspect,' said Churchill. 'How are we going to gather more evidence? Oh, I've just remembered. Wasn't the teapot which was used to murder the chief inspector being reconstructed and expertly examined in Dorchester? We need to ask Mappin if he's got anything incriminating from it.'

'It won't have Mrs Llewellyn-Dalrymple's fingerprints on it,' said Pemberley.

'What makes you so sure?'

'I remember shaking her hand when we met her at the retirement party. She was wearing gloves.'

Chapter Thirty-Seven

CHURCHILL AND PEMBERLEY CALLED ON INSPECTOR MAPPIN the following morning.

'Where's your friend Inspector Kendall?' asked Churchill when they stepped into the police station.

'He's been called out to look at a vandalised postbox,' said Mappin. 'And the longer he stays out, the better.'

'It must be rather difficult policing when the pair of you are at loggerheads all the time.'

'It will soon get resolved, Mrs Churchill, don't worry. I feel sure Superintendent Trowelbank will be impressed once I solve this murder case.'

'And what will happen if Inspector Kendall solves it before you?'

'He won't. It's as simple as that. He's merely an empty vessel who makes a loud noise.'

'Yes, I agree with that description. Anyway, Miss Pemberley and I are here to report a crime.'

'Really?' He rubbed his brow. 'What's happened now?'

'Our Austin Seven Chummy Tourer was stolen while parked outside this police station yesterday. It's now parked

The Teapot Killer

on Mr Letcher's garage forecourt and has been painted a lurid shade of orange.'

'Oh dear. So Letcher's up to his old tricks again.'

'And he's admitted it too.'

'Right, well I shall have a word with him, Mrs Churchill, and seize that motor car.'

'Thank you. And while we're here, Inspector, can I ask if any fingerprints have been retrieved from the teapot which was used in Chief Inspector Llewellyn-Dalrymple's murder?'

'As I recall, the results were fairly inconclusive.'

Inspector Mappin retrieved his notebook from his jacket pocket and leafed through it. 'Here we are. The only fingerprints retrieved from the teapot were those belonging to the owner of the teapot, Mrs Honeypear.'

Churchill's heart sank. 'I see. That's interesting because Miss Pemberley recalls Mrs Llewellyn-Dalrymple was wearing gloves on the day of her husband's murder. If she murdered him with the teapot, then she wouldn't have left any fingerprints on it.'

Inspector Mappin gave a laugh. 'I think it's highly unlikely she murdered her own husband, ladies.'

'You don't think so?'

'No.'

'You don't think she would have been angry he was having an affair with Mrs Honeypear?'

Inspector Mappin gasped. 'Llewellyn-Dalrymple was having an affair with Mrs Honeypear? I don't believe it. He wouldn't have done something like that.'

'Mrs Honeypear admitted it to us herself,' said Churchill. 'And what's more, Mr Letcher has photographs of them together. That's why he had such a hold over Chief Inspector Llewellyn-Dalrymple. He threatened to show the photographs to his wife. It was an empty threat though, because it turned out that Mrs Llewellyn-Dalrymple knew about the affair, anyway.'

Inspector Mappin shook his head and wiped his brow some more. 'This is all rather a lot of information to take in at once, Mrs Churchill. I shall have a word with Mr Letcher and ask to see those photographs. I'll also see what I can do about your car. But despite all this, I absolutely refuse to believe Mrs Llewellyn-Dalrymple had anything to do with her husband's death, so you can forget that theory for now.'

He was interrupted by his telephone ringing.

'Good morning, Inspector Mappin speaking.' His face paled. 'Oh goodness… right… I shall be there in a jiffy.'

He slowly replaced the telephone receiver, his expression ashen.

'Is everything alright, Inspector?'

'No, it's not. I'm afraid there's been another murder.'

Chapter Thirty-Eight

'Who's the victim, Inspector?' asked Churchill.

Mappin gave a sigh. 'Farmer Drumhead.'

Churchill gasped. 'No! I refuse to believe it! Why would anyone want to harm Farmer Drumhead?'

'I don't know, but I'm going to catch them.' He got to his feet and put on his inspector's cap. 'I've just about had enough of all this!'

A little while later, Churchill, Pemberley and Oswald waited by the gate of Farmer Drumhead's farm for news. A small crowd had gathered, anxious for an update.

Eventually, Inspector Mappin and Inspector Kendall emerged from the farm and walked up to the gate.

Inspector Mappin cleared his throat. 'I'll tell you all what's happened and then you can clear off and give the Drumhead family some peace. Understandably, they are deeply distressed by this incident, as am I. I knew Farmer Drumhead for many years.'

'And I only met him for the first time a few days ago,' added Inspector Kendall. 'But he seemed a very nice man.'

Inspector Mappin glared at him, then continued, 'Farmer Drumhead was found in a barn this morning by one of his workers, Fred Beanfork. He appears to have been hit over the head by a shovel.'

There were cries of shock from the crowd.

'It's very upsetting indeed,' said Mappin. 'And there was absolutely no justification for violence of this sort. So please be assured that I will work my absolute hardest to bring the perpetrator to justice.'

'And so will I,' said Inspector Kendall. 'With my valuable experience on the streets of Salisbury, I will bring a lot of expertise to this investigation.'

Inspector Mappin rolled his eyes.

'Did anyone see the suspect?' called out someone.

'No,' said Mappin. 'No one saw anyone running away from the scene—not that we know of yet. Obviously, we'll continue to speak to people who were in the vicinity at the time and find out if they saw anything. But this happened fairly early this morning, shortly after Farmer Drumhead began his work for the day. When Fred Beanfork discovered him, he'd probably already been there for a little while. Now off you all go, we have a lot of work to do.'

The crowd dispersed and everyone began to walk back towards the village.

A heavy sadness weighed on Churchill. 'I don't understand why Farmer Drumhead would be attacked like this. He never bothered anyone.'

'It's interesting that Fred Beanfork found him,' said Pemberley. 'He could have been the one who committed the attack.'

'Sadly, I think you could be right, Pembers. He's already a suspect in Chief Inspector Llewellyn-Dalrymple's murder, and he could have driven that tractor at Inspector Mappin. But why would he turn on his boss? That's the bit that doesn't make sense to me. Let's call on Mrs Beanfork and find out what she has to say about all this.'

'It's terrible!' said Mrs Beanfork. 'Fred is desperately upset about it!'

Churchill and Pemberley stood with her in her parlour. Pemberley held Oswald in her arms and the Beanfork cats eyed them from their resting places.

'Please move a cat and sit down,' said Mrs Beanfork.

Churchill and Pemberley hesitated.

'Oh very well, I'll do it.' She lifted a shaggy silver-haired cat from an armchair and put it on the coffee table. Then she picked up a white cat who gave a resentful miaow. 'Oh George, you're always so grumpy. Just let the ladies sit down somewhere.' She put George on the hearthrug, and he walked away with his nose in the air.

'Fred!' called out Mrs Beanfork as she picked up a ginger tabby from her chair. 'Come and join us!'

'I didn't realise he was here,' said Churchill.

'Oh yes, he was too upset about this morning's discovery to continue with his day's work. And besides, he doesn't have a boss anymore!'

Fred shuffled into the room, holding a mug of tea in his hand. A thin cigarette end hung from his lip.

'What an awful morning you've had,' Churchill said to him. 'Did you have to speak to the police too?'

The young man nodded. 'I had to speak to Mappin first, and then I had to say the same thing all over again to Kendall. I didn't even have much to say. I just arrived at the barn this morning, and there he was, lying on the ground with the shovel next to him.'

'How awful for you! I can't understand why anyone would want to harm Farmer Drumhead.'

'I don't understand it either. Everyone liked him.'

'Had he had a disagreement with anyone who worked on the farm recently?'

Fred shook his head. 'He was angry that someone took his tractor and drove it into Inspector Mappin's garden. He had a word with all of us about it and we all denied it, of course, because none of us did it.'

'It really is terrible,' said Churchill. 'It's astonishing that no one's been able to find out who drove that tractor yet, and I can understand why Farmer Drumhead thought it was someone who worked on his farm.'

'But it wasn't,' said Fred. 'It was none of us. Someone got onto the farm and did it.'

'I've just thought of a possibility,' said Pemberley. 'Maybe Farmer Drumhead did discover who drove that tractor into Inspector Mappin's garden.'

'Perhaps he did!' said Churchill. 'Do you think he confronted the person?'

Pemberley nodded. 'Yes, I think that's what could have happened. He confronted the person, and now they've murdered him to keep him quiet.'

'Oh!' Mrs Beanfork clasped her hands to her face in horror. 'And to think that my son could have got caught up in that, too. It's just horrendous!'

Mrs Beanfork and her son seemed suitably upset about Farmer Drumhead's murder, but Churchill couldn't make up her mind about them. Were they genuinely upset? Or were they very good actors?

Chapter Thirty-Nine

'I FEEL LIKE A DARK CLOUD HAS DESCENDED ON ME TODAY,' said Churchill once she and Pemberley had left the Beanforks's home. 'Shall we cheer ourselves up with lunch at the tea rooms?'

'I've already arranged to meet Miss Applethorn for lunch in the tea rooms today,' said Pemberley.

'Oh, have you? Well, that will be nice for you.'

Churchill debated whether she should still go to the tea rooms, knowing that Pemberley and her new friend would be there. But she really wanted some sandwiches and cake and thought it would be silly to deny herself them just because Pemberley had made other plans.

Pemberley went off with Oswald to call on Miss Applethorn and Churchill made her way to the tea rooms alone. She sat herself at a table in the window.

'Hello Mrs Churchill and thank you for reuniting me with my cousin, Mrs Thonnings,' said Mrs Honeypear. 'We had little to do with each other when I was growing up because she was so much older than me. But we've actually discovered we have a great deal in common and I feel like we're already old friends.'

'That's lovely to hear,' said Churchill, feeling cheered by the news.

She had just started on her cheese and cucumber sandwiches when Pemberley and Miss Applethorn entered the tea rooms.

'Oh, hello, Mrs Churchill,' said Pemberley. 'Are you enjoying your sandwich?'

'Very much so. And hello, Miss Applethorn.'

Miss Applethorn gave her a polite smile, and the pair went off to sit at another table.

Churchill quietly ate her sandwich and tried not to listen in on Pemberley and Miss Applethorn's conversation. They were discussing dog training tips, and she thought it all sounded rather dull. Outside the tea rooms, she could see Oswald and Whisker patiently waiting for their owners.

Mrs Thonnings entered the tea rooms and cast a glance at Churchill before turning to Pemberley and Miss Applethorn, then back to Churchill again. She frowned and lowered herself into the chair opposite Churchill. 'Have you and Miss Pemberley fallen out?' she asked.

'No, we haven't fallen out at all, Mrs Thonnings. She's just having tea with her new friend, Miss Applethorn.'

'And they've not asked you to join them?'

'No. But that's because they're discussing things like training dogs.'

'Well, I think it's rather rude of them not to invite you all the same.'

'To be honest with you, Mrs Thonnings, I'm quite glad they haven't asked me. I would find the conversation extremely boring.'

'Well, so would I, actually. Perhaps you'd like me to join

you instead, Mrs Churchill? Unless you prefer not to have company at the moment.'

Churchill gave a sad sniff and sipped her tea.

'Actually, some company would be very nice, Mrs Thonnings. Thank you.'

Chapter Forty

After lunch, Churchill returned to the office and updated the incident board. She used pieces of string to link Chief Inspector Llewellyn-Dalrymple with Inspector Mappin and Farmer Drumhead.

'Three attacks,' she said to herself. 'And two of them fatal. Who's behind this?'

She looked at each suspect in turn: Mrs Beanfork, Fred Beanfork, Mrs Honeypear, Mr Letcher and Mrs Llewellyn-Dalrymple. 'There are still too many suspects,' she said. 'How are we going to narrow them down?'

She sat down at her desk and took out her notebook and pen. She chewed the end of her pen as she thought. 'I have to solve this,' she said. 'But how?'

An hour later, Churchill had filled her notebook with copious notes. She was just thinking about putting the kettle on when Pemberley and Oswald returned.

'Sorry I took a little longer, Mrs Churchill,' said Pemberley. 'Miss Applethorn and I have decided Oswald and Whisker need to get more exercise, so we decided to take them for a walk.'

The Teapot Killer

'I see. Well, I enjoyed the peace and quiet to be honest with you, Pembers. I've had a good opportunity to think about the murder case.'

'That's good to hear. Have you—'

A frantic knock at the door interrupted them and frizzy-haired Mrs Beanfork fell into the office, gasping.

'Oh good grief,' said Churchill, leaping to her feet. 'Whatever is the matter?' She helped her to a chair.

'It's Fred,' she gasped, clutching her chest. 'They've arrested him again!'

'Who has?'

'Inspector Mappin,' said Mrs Beanfork. 'And he's accusing him of murdering Farmer Drumhead and Chief Inspector Llewellyn-Dalrymple and driving a tractor at him. But my Fred's innocent! He didn't do it!'

'Oh dear,' said Churchill.

'I'll make an emergency cup of tea,' said Pemberley.

'Good idea, Miss Pemberley. I'll get the emergency biscuits.'

A few moments later, Mrs Beanfork was able to speak a little more.

'Inspector Mappin came for him this afternoon. Fred swears he's innocent and I believe him! I know he was angry at Chief Inspector Llewellyn-Dalrymple because he was jailed for three years, but once he got out of prison and was happy working for Farmer Drumhead, he wanted to forget all about the past and get on with his life. Perhaps even find himself a nice wife and settle down and have some children. That was all he wanted! He would never have ruined everything by murdering people. Especially Farmer Drumhead! He was the man who gave him another chance when no one else would!'

She sobbed into her handkerchief.

'How terrible for you, Mrs Beanfork,' said Churchill. 'Let's calm down with a cup of tea and some biscuits.'

'Please will you speak to Inspector Mappin for me? I would go but I'm too upset!'

Churchill and Pemberley exchanged a glance. 'Alright,' said Churchill. 'We will.'

Once Mrs Beanfork was feeling more recovered, Churchill and Pemberley left their office to visit the police station.

As they stepped outside, they found a brown Austin Seven Chummy Tourer.

'Oh good grief, Pembers. Who's parked their car here? It's almost blocking our door.'

'Just a moment,' said Pemberley. 'That's Cousin Bertie's car.'

'It can't be. It's brown.'

'Yes, and it was recently painted orange, wasn't it? Mr Letcher was clearly trying to paint it blue again, but it hasn't worked, and he's now mixed up blue and orange and made brown. I know it's the same car because it's got its usual number plate on it again.'

'Oh goodness, Pemberley, it looks awful. It's a disgusting colour. We're going to have to ask Mr Letcher to have another go at it.'

'I actually quite like it,' said Pemberley. 'It's like the colour of coffee cake.'

'Whenever I look at a motor car, Pembers, cake is the last thing I think about.'

'But if you think of coffee cake, Mrs Churchill, you might grow to like it.'

'You don't think Cousin Bertie is going to be annoyed his car is now brown?'

'No, I think he'll quite like it too.'

Churchill sighed. 'Very well. At least Letcher has returned it. Let's hop in and drive to the police station.'

'Hello, Mrs Churchill,' said Inspector Mappin. 'I don't have much time to talk now, I've got to interview young Fred Beanfork, who's being held in the cells.'

'I've just had a visit from his mother,' said Churchill. 'She's extremely upset.'

'Yes, I expect she is,' said the inspector. 'Mothers rarely like their sons being arrested.'

'What makes you think young Fred Beanfork is responsible?'

'He was in the vicinity of all three attacks, Mrs Churchill. He was at my retirement party—'

'So was the entire village,' said Churchill.

'He was working on Farmer Drumhead's farm when a tractor was driven down the hill at me in an attempt to end my life. And he discovered Farmer Drumhead's body in the barn. At least, that's what he told us. But if you ask me, Mrs Churchill, I think he could have carried out the deed himself. He has no alibi for the time when the tractor was driven down the hill, and his presence at the scene of Farmer Drumhead's murder tells you all you need to know.'

Although Churchill realised it didn't look good for Fred Beanfork, she felt the need to challenge Inspector Mappin's theory. 'This is merely circumstantial, Inspector,' she said. 'What motive could Fred have had?'

'He doesn't like police officers, that's for sure.'

'That's because he was imprisoned for three years for something he didn't do.'

'A jury found him guilty of the robbery, Mrs Churchill.

It's quite obvious the young man has always had a criminal side to him.'

'But you don't have any other evidence, Inspector.'

'Oh, I will have before long, Mrs Churchill. Now, I don't know why you're bothering me about this. I've got the murderer now, so the case is solved.'

Churchill, Pemberley and Oswald got back into the car.

'I realise Fred Beanfork is suspicious,' said Churchill. 'But I don't think he's the murderer.'

'Why not?' asked Pemberley.

'Because I believed his mother earlier when she told us how much he wanted to get on with his new life. I think she's right. After three years in prison, I don't think he would have jeopardised his freedom.'

They drove along the high street a short distance before Pemberley brought the car to an abrupt halt. Churchill was jerked forward in her seat. 'What are you doing, Pemberley?'

'Litter,' she replied, getting out of the car. 'I can't bear it when people just drop something in the street. Why not put it in the bin? There's one right outside the tea rooms.'

Pemberley picked up the piece of offending rubbish and walked over to the bin. She scowled, then returned to the car with the rubbish still in her hand.

'What's the matter now?' asked Churchill.

'I can't put it in the bin. It's full.'

'So that's why someone dropped it in the street. What is it?'

'A lolly wrapper.'

'It's unusual for the bin to be full, the council are usually quite good at emptying it.'

'I know,' said Pemberley. 'But someone's put a pair of boots in there.'

'A pair of boots? Let me see.' Churchill got out of the car and walked over to the bin. 'Why would someone throw these out?' she said. 'They're not even badly worn. Someone could make good use of these.'

She lifted the boots out of the bin.

'Oh yuck,' said Pemberley. 'I can't say I'd want to handle someone's old muddy boots.'

Churchill turned one of the boots over and examined the sole. 'Look at the thick tread on these boots, Pemberley. I recognise it. We saw this exact same tread in the flower bed next to Inspector Mappin's trampled tulips!'

'Really?'

'Yes. I made a sketch in my notebook, didn't I?' She pulled her notebook out of her handbag and turned to the sketch of the footprint. 'It matches! It's the same boot!'

Pemberley gasped. 'The driver of the tractor must have realised he left his footprints behind. He wanted to get rid of the boots before anyone could link them to him.'

'He may have discarded some other things at the same time,' said Churchill. Cautiously, she peered into the bin to see what else was in there. 'What have we got here? Goodness, I don't believe it.' She reached in and pulled out a piece of card. 'It's a menu from the tea rooms. And not just one either, there are about a dozen of them in here. It's as if someone decided to discard a pair of boots and a pile of tea shop menus in the bin.' She turned to look at the tea rooms. 'Let's go and see what Mrs Honeypear makes of this. Perhaps she intended to throw her menus in this bin. But I wonder if she saw who put the boots in there?'

'Excuse me,' said a man on a bicycle. 'Does that motor car belong to you? It's blocking the entire street.'

'Oh yes. Sorry about that,' said Pemberley. 'We got distracted. I'll park it properly.'

Once Pemberley had parked the car sensibly, they went into the tea rooms.

'Hello, ladies!' said Mrs Honeypear. 'Tea?'

'Well, I don't see why not,' said Churchill. 'We're in here, so we may as well have some. And some chocolate cake as well, please, Mrs Honeypear. By the way, I found one of your old menus in the bin outside.'

'Yes,' said Mrs Honeypear. 'I threw out a bunch of old menus this morning. I've had some new ones made, and those ones were getting very tatty.'

'I see,' said Churchill. 'I don't suppose you saw who put these boots in there as well, did you?'

'Oh yes, I put them in there,' said Mrs Honeypear. 'My bin out the back is full.'

Churchill felt surprised. 'The boots belonged to you, Mrs Honeypear?'

'No, they're not mine. Someone left them in my doorway. When I arrived this morning, they were just sitting there. I didn't know what else to do with them, so I threw them out.'

'Interesting,' said Churchill. 'The soles of these boots match a footprint at the scene of the tractor attack on Inspector Mappin. If you don't mind, I'm going to hand them to him.'

Mrs Honeypear bit her lip. 'You're going to give the boots to the police?'

'Yes,' said Churchill. 'I believe they've been used in a crime.'

'Very well,' said Mrs Honeypear. 'If you must. I'll go and fetch your tea and cake.'

Churchill lowered her voice once Mrs Honeypear was out of earshot. 'Goodness, Pembers. This is all very suspicious. Did you notice her subdued reaction when I told her we were going to give the boots to the police? And do you really think someone left them outside her door? It seems an odd thing to do.'

'It does seem odd,' said Pemberley. 'She could have worn those boots to drive that tractor down the hillside and then run away in them. By wearing men's boots, she could have intended to mislead the police into thinking they were looking for a man. And then she flung them in the bin, hoping no one would see them.'

'But she made the mistake of discarding them in a bin close to her place of business,' said Churchill. 'Why would she do that? I really don't know what to make of this at all.'

'If Mrs Honeypear is the murderer,' said Pemberley, 'then she wouldn't admit to putting the boots in the bin, would she? She would deny ever having had anything to do with them.'

'That's a fair point, Pembers. But she doesn't know we know about the footprints in the flower bed, does she? She probably doesn't think there's any harm in admitting it to us.'

'Or she could be telling the truth,' said Pemberley. 'It's possible someone left those boots by her doorway in order to frame her.'

Churchill nodded. 'Yes, that's also possible. All we can do now is take these boots to Inspector Mappin and tell him our findings.'

They returned to the police station once they'd finished their tea.

'Mappin is interviewing young Beanfork,' said Inspector Kendall. He glanced at the boots in her hand. 'What have you found there, Mrs Churchill?'

'A pair of boots which we believe were used by the person who drove the tractor at Inspector Mappin.'

He raised an eyebrow. 'Is that so? And how did you come by those?'

'We found them in the bin outside the tea rooms. Mrs Honeypear said she put them there.'

'Mrs Honeypear put them there? How strange.'

'She says someone left them by her door.'

'And what makes you think these boots were used in the attack on Inspector Mappin?'

'The tread on the sole matches the footprint which was found in Inspector Mappin's tulip bed. If Mrs Honeypear is to be believed, someone left the boots outside her door.'

'And if she's not to be believed?'

'Then that means she could have worn them when she drove a tractor at Inspector Mappin. But I can't imagine it. She has dainty little feet and these boots are enormous.'

'Nothing that extra pairs of socks can't solve.' He got to his feet and put on his cap. 'I'll go and speak to her now.'

'Why you? Why not Inspector Mappin?'

'He's busy with young Beanfork, as I've already told you. Now leave the boots with me and I'll deal with it.'

'I don't want Inspector Kendall investigating,' said Pemberley once they'd left the station. 'He's a waste of space.'

'I agree,' said Churchill. 'But he has a point. Inspector Mappin is busy with Fred Beanfork. Regrettably, I think we have to let Inspector Kendall investigate. And who knows? Perhaps he'll surprise us and find out who those boots belong to.'

Chapter Forty-One

'I REALISED LATE LAST NIGHT THAT WE'VE FORGOTTEN ALL about Mr Letcher,' Churchill said to Pemberley the following morning. They were drinking tea and eating ginger biscuits. 'He returned Cousin Bertie's motor car to us after stealing it, but has he been arrested for theft? No! He's just free to carry on with whatever he pleases. I need to speak to Mappin about it.'

'Inspector Mappin is busy with Fred Beanfork.'

'I realise that. And I'm also fairly certain Fred Beanfork is not the murderer. Mappin has his priorities wrong and— oh, would you look at that! My cardigan is missing a button. When did that happen?'

Churchill glanced at the floor around her desk and chair. 'I can't see it anywhere. Oh, bother.'

'You could get a replacement from Mrs Thonnings,' suggested Pemberley.

'Yes, I could. And I shall do that now because I shall be too busy to do it later.' Churchill picked up her handbag and got to her feet. 'I'll be back soon, Pemberley. You can have the last ginger biscuit if you like.'

. . .

Mrs Thonnings looked cheery as she stood behind the counter of her haberdashery shop. 'Thank you again, Mrs Churchill, for reacquainting me with my cousin, Mrs Honeypear. She came to mine for dinner last night, and we had an absolutely wonderful time together.'

'Well, that's delightful,' said Churchill. She hoped Mrs Honeypear wasn't the murderer. Otherwise, Mrs Thonnings's budding relationship with her cousin was going to be short-lived.

'You're such a clever old thing, Mrs Churchill,' continued the haberdasher. 'It never occurred to me we actually shared the same grandmother. And now it makes complete sense why our recipes were identical. I feel so terribly bad for accusing Mrs Honeypear of theft. But fortunately, she's been quite understanding.'

'That's fortunate,' said Churchill. 'I wonder if you could help me find a replacement button for this cardigan, Mrs Thonnings? I've lost one.'

'Oh dear. Yes, I'm sure I've got some identical ones. Let me find them for you.'

They were looking through the buttons when the bell above the door tinkled and two ladies strolled in. Churchill recognised the haughty face of Mrs Llewellyn-Dalrymple, but not the lady she was with.

'This is the lovely little haberdashery shop I was telling you about, Mrs Trowelbank,' said Mrs Llewellyn-Dalrymple.

'What a delightful little place,' said her companion. She had a nasal voice, perfectly waved hair, and wore a smart cornflower-blue coat.

Mrs Thonnings stepped over to them. 'Hello, Mrs Llewellyn-Dalrymple. How can I help you today?'

'I thought I'd show Mrs Trowelbank your shop. She doesn't come to Compton Poppleford very often. She lives in Dorchester. But I maintain your haberdashery shop is far better than the one in Dorchester.'

'Do you really, Mrs Llewellyn-Dalrymple? Oh, that's wonderful to hear! You're one of my favourite customers!' Churchill felt her toes curl as she listened. 'Feel free to have a look around, ladies. And if there's anything I can help you with, Mrs Trowelbank, don't hesitate to ask.'

Mrs Llewellyn-Dalrymple caught Churchill's eye and gave her an icy stare. Churchill pursed her lips and chose to say nothing.

The two ladies went off to another part of the shop, discussing quilting needles.

Churchill whispered to Mrs Thonnings. 'You do realise Mrs Llewellyn-Dalrymple spends an awful lot of time in the company of that crook Letcher?'

'Does she?' said Mrs Thonnings. 'Well, she's not a very good judge of character, is she? However, I shan't hold it against her because she spends an awful lot of money whenever she comes into my shop. Hopefully, Mrs Trowelbank will spend just as much too. She looks as if she's worth it, doesn't she?'

'I'll take this button, Mrs Thonnings,' said Churchill. She glanced around for something else to buy, just to show she wasn't a spendthrift. 'And that pack of crochet hooks as well.'

'Are you sure you need crochet hooks, Mrs Churchill? I thought you had plenty.'

'I like to replace some from time to time,' she said.

'Well, it's quite a pricey pack. It's one shilling and six.'

'Yes, I know,' said Churchill breezily. 'But I'll take that pack and the button. Thank you, Mrs Thonnings.'

Chapter Forty-Two

INSPECTOR MAPPIN AND INSPECTOR KENDALL WERE bickering when Churchill arrived at the police station.

'I haven't helped myself to any of your paperclips, Mappin,' said Kendall.

'Well, you must have done because I had a full box of them in my drawer a few days ago and now it's only half-full.'

'You must have used them without realising.'

'And how would I have managed that? Oh, hello, Mrs Churchill.' Inspector Mappin smoothed his jacket. 'How can I help?'

'Have you arrested Mr Letcher for the theft of our motor car?'

'Ah, er... no. Not yet. I'm afraid events took over when Farmer Drumhead was murdered.'

'So you haven't arrested him for stealing our car?'

Mappin scratched the back of his head. 'Well... I did.'

'And what happened?'

He pulled at his ear. 'I had to let him go again.'

'Why?'

'Because there was no evidence.'

'No evidence, Inspector? The car that was stolen from us was put up for sale on his own garage forecourt!'

'He denied he knew it was stolen.'

'Oh he did, did he? Who did he get the car from?'

'He told me it was an associate of his, but he didn't want to reveal names because he's fearful of reprisals.'

'That's a very convenient defence.'

'I realise it looks a little bit fishy. But I had instructions from up high that he should be released. The case simply isn't strong enough. And you've now got your car back.'

'It's brown, Inspector.'

'If you speak to Letcher nicely, then I'm sure he'll have another go at repainting it.'

Churchill sighed. 'Who did the instructions from up high come from?'

'Superintendent Trowelbank. He telephoned me personally and explained to me I didn't have enough evidence to charge Mr Letcher. So I'm afraid I had to follow orders.'

'Oh, did you? How interesting.'

'It's the chain of command, Mrs Churchill.'

'Yes, I'm sure it is. Although I find it astonishing that Mr Letcher never gets prosecuted for anything.' She wondered if Letcher was now blackmailing Superintendent Trowelbank.

'But you'll be pleased to hear that I'm certain Fred Beanfork is the murderer who's been terrorising this village for the past fortnight.'

'Really? What makes you so convinced?'

'He left his muddy boots outside the tea rooms.'

'How do you know the muddy boots belong to him?'

'Because they fit his feet.'

'But that doesn't mean they're his boots,' said

Churchill. 'And besides, you only have Mrs Honeypear's word for it that the boots were left outside her tea rooms. They could be her boots.'

Inspector Mappin laughed. 'What on earth would Mrs Honeypear want with a large pair of muddy labourers' boots?'

'She could have put them on her feet while she drove the tractor at you, knowing she would leave footprints at the scene. What better way of misleading an investigation than wearing a pair of boots that are totally unsuitable? And besides, why would Fred Beanfork leave his boots outside the tea rooms?'

'To frame Mrs Honeypear. But it didn't work. He doesn't fool me.'

Churchill sighed again. She had a lot of work to do. And not much time before Fred Beanfork was unfairly charged with murder.

Chapter Forty-Three

CHURCHILL RETURNED TO THE OFFICE IN A PENSIVE MOOD.

'Mappin is hapless,' she said to Pemberley. 'I'm beginning to wish he'd retired after all. And Mrs Llewellyn-Dalrymple is not a mourning widow, she was swanning about in Mrs Thonnings's haberdashery shop earlier with a friend of hers.' Churchill sank into her chair. 'And she's also swanning about with the local crook who stole our motor car. Mappin tells me he can't do anything about it because there's not enough evidence!'

Pemberley shook her head. 'Life seems so unfair sometimes.'

'Yes, it does. There's something funny going on and I can't quite put my finger on it.' Churchill checked her desk drawer to see if she'd hidden an emergency eclair in there. Then she remembered she'd eaten it a few days previously.

'What's Mrs Llewellyn-Dalrymple's new friend called?' asked Pemberley.

'Mrs Trowelbank.'

'Just like Superintendent Trowelbank then.'

'Yes, it's an unusual surname, isn't it?' Churchill

paused, her eyes widening. 'Goodness me, Pembers, I've got it!'

'What have you got, Mrs Churchill?'

'Mrs Trowelbank must be the superintendent's wife! I heard Mrs Llewellyn-Dalrymple say she lives in Dorchester. That's where the superintendent is based. Yes, it's all becoming clear now…' Churchill tapped her chin as she thought. 'I'll tell you what's happening here. Letcher has persuaded Mrs Llewellyn-Dalrymple to put a good word in for him with the superintendent's wife. That's how he's avoiding justice.'

'But why would Mrs Llewellyn-Dalrymple do that for him?'

'I don't know, Pembers. Love? Money? Either way, she seems very taken with him. He has a hold over her.' Churchill felt a bitter taste in her mouth.

'But how can you be certain, Mrs Churchill?'

'I can't be completely certain… not just yet. But I think there's an awful lot of corruption going on in the Dorset Constabulary, Pembers. Fred Beanfork is likely to stand trial again for something he didn't do, and Mr Letcher is as free as a bird.' She checked her watch. 'What time is the next train to Dorchester, Pembers? I think we need to go there and make some inquiries.'

After a fruitful afternoon in Dorchester, Churchill, Pemberley and Oswald returned to Compton Poppleford on the last train.

'Let's get a little gathering together on the village green tomorrow morning, Pembers,' said Churchill. 'It's time to tell everyone what we've found out.'

Chapter Forty-Four

'What's all this about, Mrs Churchill?' asked Inspector Mappin, as everyone gathered beneath the oak tree on the village green the following morning. 'I've already caught the murderer!'

'I have some new evidence, Inspector,' said Churchill.

'What?'

'You'll see. Have you and Inspector Kendall got your handcuffs?'

'Oh yes.' He tapped them proudly where they hung on his belt. 'I always have them at the ready.'

'I think everyone's here, Mrs Churchill,' said Pemberley.

'Are they? Well, I'd better get started then.' Her hands shook as she leafed through her notebook one last time. She always got nervous at times like this. 'Is everyone ready?' she called out to the group.

Heads nodded.

'Very well. I shall begin. We're all standing close to the place where Chief Inspector Llewellyn-Dalrymple was murdered in the refreshments tent at Inspector Mappin's retirement party almost two weeks ago,' she said. 'But who committed the crime? And why?'

'Why indeed?' called out Mrs Higginbath.

'The most obvious culprit in this sorry case is Fred Beanfork,' said Churchill. 'He bore a grudge against the police force—and why wouldn't he? He spent three years in prison serving time for a crime he didn't commit. At the time of Inspector Mappin's retirement party, Mr Beanfork had only just been released from jail. Imagine how angry he must have felt when he clapped eyes on Chief Inspector Llewellyn-Dalrymple—the man who'd ensured he'd been locked away for three years. He must have felt a lot of anger towards him. As did his mother, Mrs Beanfork. In fact, she admitted to Miss Pemberley and me that she was so angry with the chief inspector that she confronted him at the retirement party. Witnesses say she hit him with her handbag, and she admits to it too. No one can blame the Beanforks for feeling anger and resentment towards the police after what they'd been through. And that anger extended to Inspector Mappin too.'

Mappin shifted from one foot to the other, looking offended.

'I'm afraid so, Inspector Mappin,' said Churchill. 'Even though it was Chief Inspector Llewellyn-Dalrymple who ensured Fred Beanfork went to prison, in the eyes of the Beanfork family, you did nothing to stop it. They were angry with everyone in the police force. So it's not impossible to imagine they may have wanted to harm both you and Chief Inspector Llewellyn-Dalrymple.

'As for Farmer Drumhead, the only motive I can think of is he witnessed Fred Beanfork driving the tractor at you, Inspector Mappin. I have little doubt Farmer Drumhead was murdered by the person who drove that tractor. He found out who it was, and unfortunately, he paid with his life. But was it Fred Beanfork who murdered him? No. And neither was it his mother, Mrs Beanfork.'

'Why not?' called out Mrs Thonnings.

'Because there are other people in the village to consider,' said Churchill. 'There's Mr Letcher. He was the reason Fred Beanfork had to spend three years in prison. The robbery at the jeweller's was committed by Mr Letcher. Mr Gilding, the jeweller, told us he thought it was him. But Chief Inspector Llewellyn-Dalrymple didn't prosecute Mr Letcher. Why? Because Mr Letcher was blackmailing him.'

This was met with gasps.

'Mr Letcher had photographs of Chief Inspector Llewellyn-Dalrymple and his mistress. He threatened to tell Mrs Llewellyn-Dalrymple about the affair unless the chief inspector was lenient on him. That's how Letcher got away with all his crimes—Chief Inspector Llewellyn-Dalrymple was too worried to prosecute him.'

'Who was he having an affair with?' asked Mrs Higginbath.

'The affair was with the owner of the tea rooms, Mrs Honeypear.'

More gasps and muttering followed. Heads turned to Mrs Honeypear who covered her face with her hands. Churchill soldiered on. 'Both Mrs Honeypear and Chief Inspector Llewellyn-Dalrymple went to great lengths to ensure their affair was kept secret. One could argue that Mrs Honeypear is a prime suspect for murdering the chief inspector. The murder took place in her refreshments tent, and the murder weapon was her own teapot. She had the perfect opportunity to attack him that day.'

'I didn't!' wailed Mrs Honeypear. 'I would never have harmed him!'

'Are you sure about that?' Churchill pressed. 'Hadn't the chief inspector assured you he would leave his wife and marry you? And had you not been waiting a few years for that to happen? You must have been growing impatient. Perhaps you finally realised that he was never going to leave his wife for you—and that made you angry?'

'No! I would have waited for him forever!'

'You say that now, Mrs Honeypear, but perhaps there was a disagreement about it in your refreshments tent that day. Perhaps you lost your temper and struck him over the head with the large stoneware teapot. Then there's the pair of muddy boots which we found in the bin outside your tea rooms. Those boots were worn by the person who drove the tractor at Inspector Mappin. You told us someone left them by your doorway, but is that really true? Perhaps you bought those boots to mislead everyone into thinking the culprit was a man. And then you carelessly disposed of them in the bin outside your business and hoped no one would notice.'

'No! It's not true!' Her lower lip wobbled.

Chapter Forty-Five

'Don't worry, Mrs Honeypear,' said Churchill. 'Although I think you had the opportunity and a motive, I don't believe you murdered Chief Inspector Llewellyn-Dalrymple.'

'So who did?' said Mrs Thonnings.

'Well, there's his wife to consider,' said Churchill. 'Mrs Llewellyn-Dalrymple knew about her husband's affair. When she told me and Mr Letcher that she knew about it, she pretended she wasn't bothered. But perhaps that was a lie. Maybe she pretended to be unbothered because she was extremely bothered. So bothered, in fact, that she hit her husband over the head with the teapot out of revenge.'

'Ridiculous!' snapped Mrs Llewellyn-Dalrymple. 'I would never have done such a thing! Yes, I knew about the affair, and I'll admit I was angry when I first found out. But I knew about it for a couple of years and I stopped caring about it. I didn't want to leave my husband because I enjoyed the status of being married to a chief inspector. That's all there is to it.'

Churchill nodded. 'How honest of you to say so, Mrs

Llewellyn-Dalrymple. But it's interesting to note that the only fingerprints found on the teapot were Mrs Honeypear's. This is to be expected, of course, because she used that teapot to serve tea that day. So either she wielded the teapot and struck the fatal blow... or you did, Mrs Llewellyn-Dalrymple—because you were wearing gloves and wouldn't have left any fingerprints on the teapot.'

More muttering ensued.

'It's obvious Mrs Honeypear did it!' shouted Mrs Higginbath.

'No! It was Mrs Llewellyn-Dalrymple!' shouted Mrs Woodbine.

'Can I urge for some quiet, please?' said Churchill. 'I need to finish my explanation. Let's return to Mr Letcher. We know he was blackmailing Chief Inspector Llewellyn-Dalrymple, and he enjoyed having full control over him. But perhaps something went wrong? Maybe the chief inspector was finally considering prosecuting him for his many crimes? Perhaps Mr Letcher's control of him was slipping?'

'You've got me all wrong, Mrs Churchill!' exclaimed Mr Letcher. 'I may have stolen your car, but I'm no murderer!'

'All the same, you do an excellent job of evading prosecution, don't you, Mr Letcher? Inspector Mappin tried arresting you for stealing our motor car. But then he received orders from Superintendent Trowelbank that he had to release you. Something's not quite right there, if you ask me. What's your hold over Superintendent Trowelbank? Are you blackmailing him, too?'

Mr Letcher shook his head. 'Absolutely not.'

'No? Then let's discuss Mrs Llewellyn-Dalrymple again,' Churchill said. 'She's good friends with the superintendent's wife. I believe you're using her friendship to protect yourself, Mr Letcher. And Mrs Llewellyn-Dalrymple—recently widowed—spends most evenings at your garage. Why? Has she fallen in love with you? Are you paying her money? What's the real story?'

'We're just friends!' Mrs Llewellyn-Dalrymple protested.

'Well, it's an odd friendship if you ask me,' said Churchill. 'And you're clearly motivated enough to put in a good word for him with Mrs Trowelbank, the superintendent's wife. It's shocking. It really is.'

'I don't understand,' said Mrs Higginbath. 'Who's the murderer?'

'Mr Letcher!' said Mrs Thonnings.

'No, it's not him,' said Churchill. 'It pains me to say it, but at the very heart of all this seedy business is corruption in the Dorset Constabulary.' She turned to Inspector Mappin. 'Chief Inspector Llewellyn-Dalrymple forced you to take retirement, didn't he, Inspector Mappin?'

He nodded. 'Yes. I actually wanted to carry on.'

'When Miss Pemberley and I spoke to your wife at your retirement party, she told us you'd been driven to despair at the thought of retirement.'

His face reddened. 'I wouldn't say it was that bad.'

'Perhaps you murdered the chief inspector so you wouldn't have to retire? It's notable how you've remained in your job as an inspector ever since the chief inspector was murdered. His death meant you could carry on happy in the job that you've always done.'

'Hear, hear!' said Inspector Kendall. 'I had little hope in you solving this, Mrs Churchill, but I think you've hit the nail right on the head!'

'And to make yourself look innocent, Inspector Mappin, perhaps you arranged for someone to drive a tractor at your garden to make it look like an attempt on your life.'

'No!' shouted Mrs Mappin, jumping to her feet. 'I refuse to believe my husband would do such a thing!'

'I wouldn't!' protested Inspector Mappin. 'None of this is true! I admit I didn't want to retire. But I would never have murdered my boss. And I certainly wouldn't have staged an attempt on my life by having someone drive a tractor at me.'

'Perhaps you paid Farmer Drumhead to drive the tractor at you,' said Churchill. 'And when he threatened to tell someone, you silenced him.'

'No! Absolutely not!'

Inspector Kendall shook his head and chuckled. 'This doesn't look good for you, Mappin.'

'Let's consider the most interesting piece of evidence Miss Pemberley and I found,' said Churchill. 'We examined the scene of Chief Inspector Llewellyn-Dalrymple's murder and found a button from a police uniform. It had the words "Dorset Constabulary" on it.'

'And I've already told you it wasn't mine,' said Mappin. 'It must have come from the chief inspector's jacket!'

'It could have done,' said Churchill. 'But there were a lot of uniformed officers at your retirement party, Inspector. It could have come from any police officer's jacket. I happen to have discovered, though, whose jacket it came from.'

'Who?' called out Mrs Thonnings.

'Tell us!' said Mrs Higginbath.

Chapter Forty-Six

'THE BUTTON AT THE CRIME SCENE CAME FROM INSPECTOR Kendall's jacket,' said Churchill.

Inspector Kendall's face fell. 'My jacket? No, that's impossible. Look, I have all my buttons!'

'Just a moment, Mrs Churchill,' said Inspector Mappin. 'Kendall and I haven't seen eye to eye over these past few weeks, but I refuse to believe that a fellow man in blue could be responsible for such awful crimes.'

'Yes, it's difficult to believe, isn't it?' said Churchill. 'That's why it took us a while to solve it. But we got there in the end.'

Inspector Kendall slapped his thigh and laughed. 'In all my career, I've never heard anything quite so funny!'

Churchill scowled at him. 'There's nothing funny about murder, Inspector Kendall.'

'But it's ridiculous! I didn't murder Chief Inspector Llewellyn-Dalrymple, I was buying an ice cream when it all happened.'

Churchill called out to the assembled crowd. 'Mrs

Higginbath,' she said. 'Did Inspector Kendall buy an ice cream from you at Inspector Mappin's retirement party?'

'Yes,' said Mrs Higginbath, stepping forward. Her thick grey hair framed her stern face.

'When?'

'When? I don't remember when.'

'Was it during the Morris dancers' performance?' asked Churchill.

'I can't remember.'

'Did you watch the Morris dancers, Mrs Higginbath?'

'Yes I did.'

'So you can't have served an ice cream to Inspector Kendall during the time of the murder,' said Churchill.

'No,' said Mrs Higginbath. 'It must have been before the Morris dancers, then.'

'Now, come on!' said Kendall. 'I arrived at the crime scene with an ice cream in my hand, don't you remember? How else could I have come by that ice cream if I hadn't just been buying it from Mrs Higginbath?'

'I remember you buying an ice cream from me,' said Mrs Higginbath. 'But I also remember watching the Morris dancers.'

'So now it's my word against Mrs Higginbath's!' said Kendall. 'I think everyone here knows the police officer is the one who should be believed.'

Mr Greystone stepped forward. 'I don't know if this could be connected to the incident or not,' he said. 'But my young granddaughter was extremely upset at Inspector Mappin's retirement party when someone snatched her ice cream from her.'

'Really?' said Churchill, shocked by how cruel someone could be. 'Do you know who it was?'

'Well, she told us a policeman did it but, of course, we didn't believe her, the poor child. We told her a policeman

The Teapot Killer

would never steal someone's ice cream but now…' He glared at Inspector Kendall. 'I realise she was telling us the truth.'

Inspector Kendall jutted his chin and avoided the undertaker's gaze.

'Shame!' called out someone.

'Shame on you!' added Mrs Thonnings.

Churchill turned to Inspector Kendall. 'Did you snatch an ice cream from a young girl to make it look like you'd been buying one at the ice cream stall when the murder occurred?'

'No! I wouldn't dream of it. All of this is nonsense. Why on earth would I murder Chief Inspector Llewellyn-Dalrymple?'

'Because you wanted his job,' said Churchill.

'I wanted his job, did I? Prove it.'

'You applied for the position of Chief Inspector three years ago, and you didn't get it, Inspector Kendall.'

His face dropped. 'And how do you know that?'

'By speaking to a nice secretary lady who works for the Dorset Constabulary. Miss Pemberley and I met with her in Dorchester yesterday.'

'Well, whoever she was shouldn't have been sharing information like that with you, Mrs Churchill,' said Mappin.

'In this case, she's been extremely helpful because she's helped us catch a murderer, Inspector,' said Churchill.

'It's all nonsense,' said Kendall. 'You can't prove anything.'

'From what I hear, you're an ambitious man,' said Churchill. 'I understand you were extremely disappointed you didn't get Chief Inspector Llewellyn-Dalrymple's job. No doubt you bore him some resentment when you failed to get it. And then, when you were moved from Salisbury to Compton Poppleford, that enraged you even more. You told Miss Pemberley and I that it was a sideways move, but really you viewed it as a step backwards in your career, didn't you?'

'A step backwards?' said Mappin. 'How offensive!'

'Chief Inspector Llewellyn-Dalrymple wanted you out, didn't he, Inspector Mappin?' said Churchill.

Mappin shifted from one foot to the other. 'Yes, I believe he did.'

'And why was that?'

'It was probably because I challenged him one too many times about his leniency on Mr Letcher,' said Mappin. 'I was called to the bank three weeks ago where Letcher was trying to cash some counterfeit cheques. I arrested him, of course, but then the chief inspector telephoned me and told me to release him. I challenged him and he overruled me. A short while later, he told me I had to take early retirement.'

'Superintendent Trowelbank then decided Inspector Kendall would replace you, Inspector Mappin,' said Churchill. 'Neither of you were happy about the change. Being moved from Salisbury to a rural backwater was too much for Inspector Kendall to handle. So he developed a rather warped plan.'

Inspector Kendall chuckled again. 'This is a great story, Mrs Churchill. All complete fiction, of course, but do continue.'

'You decided to get rid of Chief Inspector Llewellyn-Dalrymple and earn yourself the glory of solving a crime which you committed,' said Churchill. 'I don't know which innocent person you were planning to frame for it—Fred Beanfork, perhaps? Or Mrs Honeypear? That would be why you left the muddy boots by the tea rooms. Once the innocent person was framed, you could receive the credit

The Teapot Killer

for solving the murder and earn yourself a promotion at the same time. To chief inspector perhaps? After all, there was a vacancy which you had created. Unfortunately, there was something you hadn't planned for, and that was Inspector Mappin's refusal to retire. He became a thorn in your side.'

Mappin stared aghast at Kendall. 'Is this true?'

'No, of course it's not true. It's a load of codswallop.'

'But it's beginning to make sense now,' said Mappin. 'Was it really you driving that tractor at me? You wanted me out of the way?'

'Of course I wanted you out of the way, Mappin. You were supposed to be retired.'

'And I'm very glad that I stood my ground.'

'But what about poor old Farmer Drumhead?' asked Mrs Thonnings. 'Why was he murdered?'

'I suspect he realised Inspector Kendall was the man who'd stolen his tractor,' said Churchill. 'He would have confronted him, and that would have sealed his fate. Kendall had to get rid of him by attacking him with a shovel in his barn.' She shook her head. 'It's terrible. Once you murder someone to get your own way, you end up having to murder more people to cover up what you've already done. Two murders and one attempted murder. It's disgraceful.'

'It certainly is,' said Mappin. He took his handcuffs from his belt and handcuffed his colleague.

'Just a moment, Mappin, what do you think you're doing? I'm a fellow man in blue!'

'I know,' said Mappin sadly. 'And that's what makes this even worse.'

'But there's no evidence!' said Kendall. 'Is everyone just going to believe what this mad old lady has come up with?'

'There is some evidence,' said Churchill. 'After

speaking to the nice secretary lady who works for the Dorset Constabulary, we then visited the uniform department. I asked the pleasant chap there if Inspector Kendall had gone in there asking for a new button. And would you believe it? He had.'

More gasps followed.

'Well, yes,' said Kendall. 'I admit it. I needed a new button. But that button dropped off the other week when the jacket was cleaned. It doesn't mean that it came off during a struggle between me and Chief Inspector Llewellyn-Dalrymple.'

'So there was a struggle, was there?' asked Churchill.

'No! I'm speaking hypothetically.'

'Just a moment,' said Inspector Mappin. 'I've recalled something now. You were wearing gloves at my retirement party, Kendall. That's why your prints aren't on the teapot.'

'What a good observation, Inspector Mappin!' said Churchill. 'And you might want to ask around the local boot shops and find out which one Inspector Kendall bought the muddy boots from.'

'Oh yes, I shall!' Inspector Mappin grinned and turned to Kendall. 'Cut your teeth in Salisbury, did you, Kendall? Well, it didn't help you when you came to the rural backwater of Compton Poppleford, did it? You made the mistake of thinking we're all completely stupid here.'

'You are,' said Kendall bitterly. 'Except those two.' He nodded his head in the direction of Churchill and Pemberley. 'They're actually quite clever.'

Chapter Forty-Seven

'I FEEL EXHAUSTED NOW,' SAID CHURCHILL AFTER Inspector Kendall had been arrested and everyone else had dispersed. 'I'm going to take a little stroll around the duck pond. I shall see you back at the office.'

'Oh,' said Pemberley. 'Oswald and I could come with you if you like.'

'You could if you wanted to. But you usually have something planned with Miss Applethorn whenever I suggest anything these days.'

Pemberley gave a sad sniff. 'Miss Applethorn and I aren't friendly anymore.'

Churchill startled. 'Not friendly anymore? Did you have a falling out?'

'Something like that. It was all Whisker's fault. He snapped at Oswald.'

'Well, that's not very nice.'

'No, not very nice at all. And to make matters worse, Miss Applethorn blamed Oswald for it.'

'Well, that's even worse. She should have taken responsibility for her dog's behaviour.'

'Now that I think about it, that was the main problem with Miss Applethorn. She thought Whisker was perfect. She was adamant he could do nothing wrong, and on this particular occasion she accused Oswald of provoking him. Oswald has never provoked anyone in his entire little dog life.'

'No, he hasn't, Pemberley. I'm definitely taking Oswald's side on this one. It seems a shame, though, for your friendship to come to an end like this.'

'Yes, it is a shame. But with that resentment between us, it was very difficult to stay friendly.'

'I can imagine. Perhaps the dust will settle in a few days and you'll be friends again.'

'I hope not.'

'Why do you say that, Pemberley? You really liked Miss Applethorn for twelve days.'

'The argument about the dogs opened my eyes to the sort of person she really is, Mrs Churchill. She's actually quite boring.'

'You spent an awful lot of time with her, even though she was boring.'

'Initially, I thought she was interesting. But then I realised she only had five conversations, and she kept repeating them. After a while, I'd heard everything already.'

'It's very annoying when someone repeats themselves all the time. Well, let's forget about her and Whisker for now. Maybe you'll become friends again, maybe you won't. Let's go and enjoy a nice walk around the duck pond and then we can go back to the office for a cup of tea.'

'I'd like that. And we can get some fruit buns from the bakery. They're four for the price of three at the moment.'

'What a good deal.'

'I'll get six.'

The Teapot Killer

'In that deal, you'd get eight, Pembers. It's three for the price of four.'

'Four for the price of three?'

'Six then? Or eight? Oh goodness, Pemberley. I'm so confused now I don't know what to think. Let's just buy a dozen and not worry about the price.'

The End

Thank you

~

Thank you for reading this Churchill and Pemberley mystery, I really hope you enjoyed it!

Would you like to know when I release new books? Here are some ways to stay updated:

- Join my mailing list and receive the short story *A Troublesome Case*: emilyorgan.com/a-troublesome-case
- Like my Facebook page: facebook.com/emilyorganwriter
- Follow me on Goodreads: goodreads.com/emily_organ
- Follow me on BookBub: bookbub.com/authors/emily-organ
- View my other books here: emilyorgan.com

Thank you

And if you have a moment, I would be very grateful if you would leave a quick review of this book online. Honest reviews of my books help other readers discover them too!

Get a free short mystery

∼

Want more of Churchill & Pemberley? Get a copy of my free short mystery *A Troublesome Case* and sit down to enjoy a thirty minute read.

Churchill and Pemberley are on the train home from a shopping trip when they're caught up with a theft from a suitcase. Inspector Mappin accuses them of stealing the valuables, but in an unusual twist of fate the elderly sleuths are forced to come to his aid!

Visit my website to claim your FREE copy:
  emilyorgan.com/a-troublesome-case

Or scan this code:

Get a free short mystery

Also by Emily Organ

Augusta Peel Series:

Death in Soho
Murder in the Air
The Bloomsbury Murder
The Tower Bridge Murder
Death in Westminster
Murder on the Thames
The Baker Street Murders
Death in Kensington
The Dockland Murder

Penny Green Series:

Limelight
The Rookery
The Maid's Secret
The Inventor
Curse of the Poppy
The Bermondsey Poisoner

Also by Emily Organ

An Unwelcome Guest
Death at the Workhouse
The Gang of St Bride's
Murder in Ratcliffe
The Egyptian Mystery
The Camden Spiritualist

Penny Green and Emma Langley Series:

The Whitechapel Widow

Writing as Martha Bond

Lottie Sprigg Travels Mystery Series:

Murder in Venice
Murder in Paris
Murder in Cairo
Murder in Monaco
Murder in Vienna

Lottie Sprigg Country House Mystery Series:

Murder in the Library
Murder in the Grotto
Murder in the Maze
Murder in the Bay